# It Began with a Crush

*Lilian Darcy*

HARLEQUIN® SPECIAL EDITION®

Recycling programs
for this product may
not exist in your area.

ISBN-13: 978-0-373-65789-6

IT BEGAN WITH A CRUSH

Copyright © 2014 by Lilian Darcy

Printed in U.S.A.

www.Harlequin.com

*It was ridiculous how shocked she felt at seeing him, and how instinctively she'd gone back in time to when they were in high school together and she'd loathed him more than any other guy in school.*

If he ever happened to catch her looking at him after one of those smart-mouthed comments, she always glared back, just to make sure he wasn't in the slightest danger of thinking she might have a crush on him.

And now here he was in his father's dilapidated garage, where he used to help out in his teens, hands stained with engine grease, forehead lightly sheened with grimy sweat, fixing cars for a living.

She thought she should probably feel sorry for him for being here, or maybe maliciously pleased at the contrast between his openly paraded ambitions of wealth and Hollywood stardom back in high school, and the place he'd ended up. Right back where he'd started in his dad's garage.

And yet she didn't feel any of that. Instead, the emotions that washed through her were curious and empathetic and wry and—

"Life's a funny thing, huh?" Joe said quietly with a half smile, and she felt the blush heating her cheeks in reality now, not simply in her imagination. How long since she'd done that? Blushed? A hundred years?

"Um, yes. Yes, it is." She took in a dragging breath and breathed in *him,* along with the air.

Jeepers, how did the man *do* this? Less than a minute in his company and she'd already been knocked sideways by the way he looked, and even the way he *smelled,* for pity's sake.

\* \* \*

**The Cherry Sisters: Three sisters return to their childhood home in the mountains— and find the love of a lifetime!**

Dear Reader,

As I'm writing this, I've just finished Mary Jane and Joe's story, which means it's time for me to say goodbye to my three Cherry sisters and their men. I'm saying goodbye to the Adirondack region for now, also, although I may come back to it in a future book, as it's a part of the world I know and love.

I've loved writing this trilogy, and am having a hard time picking a favorite out of the three. Tucker and Daisy had all the family history to work through, which created some challenging complications. Lee and Mac had such a sizzling start to their relationship. Mary Jane and Joe have had major life disappointments to deal with and deserve some joy. I'd really like to know which is your favorite couple!

In fact, I always love to hear from readers, so don't hesitate to get in touch by email or through social media. I have a newsletter you can sign up for, which will let you know about my latest releases, and I'm on Twitter and Facebook, too.

Lilian Darcy

## Books by Lilian Darcy

### Harlequin Special Edition

*The Mommy Miracle* #2134
⌘*Daddy on Her Doorstep* #2176
⌘*A Doctor in His House* #2186
⌘*A Marriage Worth Fighting For* #2200
Ω*The One Who Changed
    Everything* #2282
Ω*The Baby Made at Christmas* #2297
Ω*It Began with a Crush* #2307

### Silhouette Special Edition

*Balancing Act* #1552
*Their Baby Miracle* #1672
¤*The Runaway and
    the Cattleman* #1762
¤*Princess in Disguise* #1766
¤*Outback Baby* #1774
*The Couple Most Likely To* #1801
*A Mother in the Making* #1880
*The Millionaire's Makeover* #1899
*The Heiress's Baby* #2063

### Silhouette Romance

*The Baby Bond* #1390
*Her Sister's Child* #1449
*Raising Baby Jane* #1478
\**Cinderella After Midnight* #1542
\**Saving Cinderella* #1555
\**Finding Her Prince* #1567
*Pregnant and Protected* #1603
*For the Taking* #1620
*The Boss's Baby Surprise* #1729
*The Millionaire's
    Cinderella Wife* #1772
*Sister Swap* #1816

Family Secrets
*Racing Hearts*

¤Wanted: Outback Wives
\*The Cinderella Conspiracy
⌘McKinley Medics
ΩThe Cherry Sisters

Other titles by Lilian Darcy
available in ebook format.

---

## *LILIAN DARCY*

has written nearly eighty books for the Silhouette Romance, Harlequin Special Edition and Harlequin Medical Romance lines. Happily married with four active children and a very patient cat, she enjoys keeping busy and could probably fill several more lifetimes with the things she likes to do—including cooking, gardening, quilting, drawing and traveling. She currently lives in Australia but travels to the United States as often as possible to visit family. Lilian loves to hear from readers. You can write to her at P.O. Box 532, Jamison P.O., Macquarie ACT 2614, Australia, or email her at lilian@liliandarcy.com.

## Chapter One

Mr. Capelli was not going to be happy.

Turning into the driveway of Capelli Auto, Mary Jane was already rehearsing her excuses. She knew her little blue car was overdue for a service, but it was the start of the summer season and they'd been so busy at Spruce Bay Resort. The car had been making a strange noise for a while, she would have to admit it, but the noise was definitely louder now than it had been at first, so it wasn't as if she'd been ignoring something so blatant all this time.

Even in her own head, it all sounded feeble, and Mr. Capelli was so good at that tolerant yet reproachful look of his. The Cherry family had been bringing their vehicles to him for service and repair for as long as she could remember.

The garage, an old-fashioned and very reassuring place, was on a quiet backstreet. Art Capelli was the kind of mechanic who told you the truth and never overcharged. He didn't deserve Mary Jane's embarrassingly neglectful attitude toward her car. Dad was always so scrupulous about maintenance, but she…

She was the worst of sinners in that department, and she knew it.

Right now, she felt as remorseful about the noise in the engine as she would have felt about bringing the vet a mangy and half-starved kitten with a splinter in its infected paw.

She parked out front of the repair shop with its brightly painted Capelli Auto sign, leaving the car windows down and the key in the ignition. There was no one in the office but she could hear sounds coming from the workshop so she went through, needing to pause for a moment or two so her eyes could adjust to the light because it was dimmer in here.

A pair of legs clad in oil-stained dark blue overalls stuck out from beneath a red pickup truck. She addressed them tentatively. "Mr. Capelli?"

There came a grunt and an inarticulate noise that probably meant, "Give me a second."

She awaited her moment of shame. Really, the noise had only gotten so bad these past few days, although it had been sounding on and off since… Oh, shoot, since her three-day spa vacation in Vermont, and that was back in mid-March, three months ago.

Problem was, when the noise occasionally stopped for a few days, she thought the car had—well—*healed* itself.

What? Cars didn't do that?

There was another grunt, and the overall-clad legs suddenly shot toward her. A pair of sturdy tan work boots fetched up inches from her shins.

"Hi, Mr—" She stopped. It wasn't Art Capelli, with his

tanned and lined sixtysomething face, his wiry gray hair and fatherly brown eyes. It was Joe, his son.

Joe, whom she hadn't seen in probably fourteen years. Longer.

Joe, with the sinfully gorgeous looks that began with his thick dark hair and ended with his perfect olive-skinned body, and encompassed pretty much every other desirable male attribute in between.

Cocky, egotistical Joe, who'd always known all too well how irresistible he was and had played on it for everything he was worth.

Possibly, she was blushing already.

"Hi," he said. They looked at each other. He lifted his head from the wheeled roller-thingy that allowed him to slide easily beneath a vehicle. "Mary Jane, right?"

"Yes."

"I saw your name in the book." And probably wouldn't have recognized her in a police lineup if he hadn't.

"Where's your dad?" she asked, and it sounded abrupt and clumsy.

He didn't answer right away, occupied with levering his strong body up off the roller-thingy so he could stand. "I'm helping him now. Taking over, really. His health isn't that great."

Once he was standing, she could see him a lot more clearly. He hadn't changed, she quickly concluded. He was every bit as good-looking as he'd been in high school. Better-looking, in fact. Her own eye for a man's looks had matured with the years, and she liked the laugh lines around his eyes and mouth, and the fine, scattered threads of silver in the short but still thick hair that framed the top half of his face.

"Right. I'm sorry to hear that," she answered him. "I

mean, that he's not well. Not sorry you're helping out. Obviously."

*Smooth, Mary Jane. Real smooth.*

There were a hundred questions she wanted to ask. What happened to the Hollywood plan? Was Joe back here for good, or just as an interim arrangement because his dad wasn't well? Wasn't there someone else who could take over the garage? What had gone wrong?

It was ridiculous how shocked she felt at seeing him, and how instinctively she'd gone back in time about eighteen years to when they were in high school together and she'd loathed him more than any other guy in school.

Yes, *loathed* him.

*Insist on that a little more, Mary Jane. Protesting too much? Never!*

She'd loathed her own reaction to him even more. He'd been so cocky back then, so magnetic and sure of himself, wearing his sense of his own sparkling future like an Armani suit. No, wait a minute. Not a suit. He was rougher than that. Make it a biker jacket, black Italian leather.

She'd tried so hard not to look at him, not to notice him, and to stay immune to the charm that oozed from him, the—what were they called, pheromones or something—that made her heart beat faster if they merely passed each other in a corridor.

The ones that made her tongue turn into a flapping fish in her mouth, and made her blush and giggle if he said something arrogant and cheeky in class. Arrogant and cheeky and usually pretty dumb, because he never did the required reading. If he ever happened to catch her looking at him after one of those smart-mouth comments, she always glared back, just to make sure he wasn't in the slightest danger of thinking she might have a crush on him.

And now here he was in his father's dilapidated garage,

where he used to help out in his teens, hands stained with engine grease, forehead lightly sheened with grimy sweat, fixing cars for a living.

While she struggled to find the right thing to say, he pulled the overalls down to his waist, laying bare a dark blue T-shirt that molded to his chest and casually showed off the toned muscles and washboard abs. He grabbed a water bottle from a benchtop and took a gulp, then took a towel and wiped it across the sweaty, grimy forehead.

She thought she should probably feel sorry for him for being here, or maybe maliciously pleased at the contrast between his openly paraded ambitions of wealth and Hollywood stardom back in high school, and the place he'd ended up. Right back where he'd started in his dad's garage.

And yet she didn't feel any of that. Instead, the emotions that washed through her were curious and empathetic and wry and—

"Life's a funny thing, huh?" Joe said quietly with a half smile, and she felt the blush heating her cheeks in reality now, not simply in her imagination. How long since she'd done that? Blushed? A hundred years?

"Um, yes. Yes, it is." She took in a dragging breath and breathed in *him,* along with the air—his slightly salt scent, his body heat, a hint of some tangy and irresistible male grooming product, and the faint odor of engine oil that should have been off-putting but for some reason wasn't.

Jeepers, how did the man *do* this? Less than a minute in his company and she'd already been knocked sideways by the way he looked, and even the way he *smelled,* for pity's sake.

She cleared her throat quickly, and there was a shift as they both pulled back onto a businesslike footing. She really was not going to ask all those questions about what he'd been doing since college and why he wasn't by this time a Hollywood heartthrob on the level of George Clooney, Bradley Cooper or Johnny Depp, or maybe a high-powered casting agent or film director.

And if she wasn't going to ask, then even less did he look as if he wanted to tell her.

"So, the car," he said. "Regular service, you said, plus you've been having a couple of problems with it?"

"It's making a noise."

He gave her his father's look, the tolerant and reproachful one, but with an additional hint of smoke that Mr. Capelli had never worn on his face in his life. Again, it took Mary Jane right back to high school and made her furious with herself. Back then, she used to think he did it on purpose—and maybe he had—because the girls fell for it like ninepins. She'd bent over backward to make sure it never worked on her.

If it was physically possible for a pair of male eyebrows and the corners of a male mouth to give the equivalent of a seductive drawl, then that was what his were doing, then and now. But today he didn't look as if he was doing it on purpose. It was just part of his face, an unconscious habit, something that betrayed a dry sense of humor.

"A noise," he said patiently.

"Yes." She tried to produce it. "*Rgrk-rgrk-rgrk.* Like that. Sort of."

To her relief, he didn't laugh, just said very plainly, "I'll take a look, and give you a call when I know what's going on."

"Uh, thanks, Cap. Yes, that would be great."

There was a silence as she realized what she'd said. *Cap.* Everyone had called him that in high school, but she had no idea if they did anymore.

He'd noticed the nickname, too. "Make it Joe," he said.

"I'm sorry."

"Cap is... Yeah. I don't go by that now."

"Sorry," she said again. And for some reason remembered something she'd learned in passing—she couldn't remember where or when—that Joe Capelli was also the name of a character in a shoot-'em-up video game.

"No big deal," the non-computer-generated Joe said. "Do you need a ride somewhere?"

"My sister's picking me up. She should be here any minute."

"I'll call you later, then, when I know what's going on with the engine."

"Thanks. Um, say hi to your dad for me. Give him my best wishes."

"Will do."

She got herself out of the grease-smelling workshop and into the June air, just as her sister Lee pulled onto the concrete apron at the front of the garage.

Lee was engaged to be married and five and a half months pregnant, beyond the tired and queasy first trimester and not yet into the big and uncomfortable third trimester, and she looked radiantly energetic, happy and alive. Her caramel-colored hair was thick and shiny in its casual ponytail, and her skin was glowing. "So what's the noise?" she said, after Mary Jane had slid into the front passenger seat.

"Don't know yet. He'll take a look at it and call to let me know."

"He must be getting pretty old for lying around under cars."

"It wasn't Mr. Capelli. It was his son. Joe."

"Joe. Wow!" Lee said. "I thought he was in Hollywood, being a movie star."

"You remember that? You were two years behind us in school."

"The whole school knew about Joe Capelli's plans. I think everyone believed in them, too."

"Really?" Mary Jane infused a watery amount of skepticism into her voice for appearance's sake, and yet she had believed in his plans just as much as everyone else. Had believed in them utterly, to the point where she looked for his face on TV or in movies for years afterward, and even once thought she'd spotted him on screen, playing a gangster's henchman who died under dramatic movie gunfire without speaking a line.

"Don't you remember him in *West Side Story?*" Lee said. "Every girl in the audience was practically moaning out loud."

"Not me."

"Well, you weren't the moaning type. I never understood why he hadn't gotten the lead role."

"Because he couldn't sing in the right range," Mary Jane answered. "He's a baritone, not a tenor."

"You *do* remember."

"But you're right, I wasn't the moaning type," Mary Jane hastened to emphasize. "I couldn't stand him."

"He did think he was God's gift to womankind, I seem to remember. Bit of a joke where he's ended up, compared to what he planned."

"Not a joke. And not the end, either. He's only thirty-five."

"Now you're defending him."

"Because I'm sure he must know what everyone is thinking," Mary Jane retorted. "He was a bit of a jerk, maybe, a bit arrogant and cocky, but he doesn't deserve that. He wasn't a bad person, just…"

"Way too much ego. Isn't that almost the definition of

jerk? You mean he doesn't deserve people thinking that being back in his father's garage is a far cry from what he expected?"

"From what we all expected."

"I know what you mean. When some people say, 'I'm gonna be a star!' you roll your eyes, but with him…"

"We were rolling our eyes for other reasons," Mary Jane agreed.

"The arrogance."

"Exactly. I never doubted he'd make it big."

Just as she'd never doubted her own future—no grand ambitions, in her case, just the usual one—the triple play of decent marriage, beautiful and welcoming home, healthy kids. Enough of a win in the lottery of life for anyone, she'd always considered.

So far, she'd scored just one out of the three.

A few minutes later, Lee turned into the driveway that led to Spruce Bay Resort and Mary Jane thought she could hardly ask for a more beautiful place to live, surrounded by pristine white snow in winter and glorious views of mountain and forest and lake in spring, summer and fall.

And yet she would have exchanged it in a heartbeat for a two-bedroom apartment over a dingy little store if it meant she got the decent marriage and healthy kids instead.

It was embarrassing. Painfully embarrassing. Way more embarrassing than Joe Capelli working in his dad's old-fashioned garage.

Incredibly embarrassing that she wanted something so outwardly ordinary and conventional and yet still it hadn't happened.

Embarrassing…and painful…and horrible…that she could feel the bitterness kicking in. She had to try *so hard,* sometimes, not to mind that both her younger sisters were now happily in love, married or engaged, with babies on the way.

She had a secret little chart tucked away in her head, and mentally awarded herself a gold star for every day she went without feeling jealous, or saying something pointed and mean, or wallowing in regret.

And even though the mental chart had quite a few gold stars on it, she hated that it existed in the first place, and no matter how much she'd disliked…well, tried to dislike… "Cap" Capelli in high school, she understood so well what he'd meant when he'd said with that wry drawl and quirked mouth, "Life's a funny thing."

Mary Jane Cherry was one of those women who looked way better at thirty-five than she'd looked at eighteen, Joe decided.

In high school, she'd had frequent skin breakouts and an orthodontic plate and puppy fat, and her hair had been an indifferent brownish color, worn too long. Now she had it cut to shoulder-length in bouncy layers with professional blond highlights, her skin was smooth, dewy and well cared for and the puppy fat had turned into a kind of ripeness that looked warm and inviting, along with the soft creases at the corners of her eyes and the smile lines around her mouth.

It was a little disturbing that he remembered her so well, but then, he'd made an extensive study of girls in high school. If he went to a reunion—which, to be clear, he had no intention of ever doing—it would probably turn out that he remembered them all.

Joe listened to Mary Jane's car engine, heard "the noise" and knew she should have brought it in for a checkup about five hundred miles ago. He did some further exploration

and diagnosis, and came up with at least three major re-
pairs that the car needed right now.

Mary Jane was lucky it had held up this far, and hadn't
left her stranded somewhere with smoke billowing from
the engine. He would need to order parts from the dis-
tributor, and when they arrived he'd need to pull apart the
whole engine to put them in. It was Tuesday today. She
wasn't getting the car back before Friday at the earliest.

He did a grease and oil change on another car, and then
a wheel alignment and a tire rotation on a third, knowing that both clients would be back soon to pick up their
vehicles. The bad-news phone call to Mary Jane would
have to wait.

Which was a pity, because it gave him more time to
think about her.

How well she'd held up in the looks and youthfulness
department. How surprised he was that she was still here.
She'd been intelligent, articulate, hard-working, always
earned good grades. He somehow would have expected
her to have moved away, in search of wider horizons.

In high school, the girls had been divided into two
groups—the ones who thought he was gorgeous and had
wild crushes on him, and the ones who thought he was
gorgeous and couldn't stand him.

Naturally, Mary Jane was in the second group, and naturally, he had been all about the girls in the first.

He'd dated—hell, he couldn't remember—at least five
or six of them. The prettiest and wildest and most popular, because those were the ones you could get the farthest
with, and were the ones that made the other guys look at
you with envy and respect, cementing your position as the
coolest kid in school.

Looking back, he could see how much he'd been riding
for a fall. Sometimes, he wanted to reach back in time and

slap his teenage self upside the head. Hard. He could also see that if just a few things had gone differently, the fall might never have happened.

Because he'd come so close.

Seriously close.

Even now, he might easily have been starring in some long-running TV crime show, or choosing between movie scripts that had Oscar potential written into every line. As he'd said to Mary Jane, life was a funny thing.

There had been a major series of audition callbacks where he'd ended up in the running, along with just one other guy, for the lead role in a crime drama series, and the other guy—now a household name—had gotten the gig. There had been one gorgeous female smile that he'd caught in a crowded diner and had followed up on instead of letting it slide.

Just those two events, and his whole life had gone off on a completely different track from the one he'd envisaged.

He couldn't let himself think about it, because on the one hand, he'd fallen so far short, but on the other, there were two things about his life now that were so incredibly precious he couldn't imagine himself without them.

The owners of the other cars showed up both at the same time, and he took their money and returned their keys and remembered he still hadn't called Mary Jane Cherry, even though it was nearly four o'clock. He was just about to pick up the phone when his father came in, towing two identical seven-year-old girls and looking pretty tired.

The girls, of course, were Joe's two precious things.

"You're going to tell me it's easier fixing cars than taking care of these two," he told his dad.

"Nah, we had a great day." But a tiring one. Dad couldn't gloss over that.

"What did you do?"

"Played on the beach at the lake. Did a round of mini golf up at that place with all the waterfalls. Had ice cream."

Dad couldn't keep up this pace all summer. He had prostate cancer, and the only good thing about this was the doctor's promise that it would kill him so slowly he'd likely die of something else first, fifteen years from now.

Joe was starting not to believe the doctor, but maybe it was the sheer energy of two little girls that had Dad looking so tired today. "I'll get them into a vacation program," he promised his father. "Day camp, or something."

"Horseback riding camp?" said both girls together, in identical and intensely hopeful voices.

Joe sighed. "Maybe horse-riding camp. We'll look into it."

He didn't know where this horsey thing was coming from, but it was *rabid.* The girls had a shared subscription to a pony magazine, and the walls of their room were covered in horsey pictures. They had a whole shelf of horsey books. Not just stories, but books on how to ride and groom and look after your pony. They had a plastic pony play-set, and plush ponies that they slept with every night, and unicorn socks—apparently unicorns counted as ponies—as well as horseshoe bracelets and pony T-shirts and pony pajamas.

Now that he and the girls had left California and come back east, it might actually be possible for them to meet a pony or two, face-to-face.

"You don't have to shove 'em into some day-camp program just because of me," Dad said.

"Pony camp! Pony camp!" said the girls.

"Well, I won't, not unless it's one they enjoy," Joe promised, but he knew he might be stretching the truth.

They might be forced to enjoy it whether they wanted to or not, because Dad really could not look after the girls all summer, five and a half days a week. The whole idea of Joe being here in the garage was to give Dad a break until they decided whether to sell the place or close it down. His taking care of the girls was a stopgap measure until the three of them got settled, because they'd only moved from California two weeks ago and still weren't fully unpacked.

Holly and Maddie had spent half their lives in day care and day camp in the four years since Joe had had full custody, because he'd had no other choice in the matter. Even so, all the child care was still way better than what they'd had before they'd come to him. He'd spared Dad most of the details on that, and it was cute...and warming, somehow...that Dad, in his innocence, viewed professional child care as such a poor option.

He would try to get a little more of the unpacking done tonight after Dad and the girls had gone to bed, he promised himself, so that at least his father didn't have to deal with the mess. Joe didn't really have time to devote a whole precious evening to going through cardboard boxes. He had studying to do. But if he didn't take care of Dad...

"Ready to close up shop?" Dad asked now, betraying his eagerness to get home and take it easy.

"Not quite. I have a phone call to make, and she's probably going to want the loaner car, so I'll have to arrange that. Why don't you take them home and put them in front of TV, while you get a break? If they've had ice cream, they won't be hungry."

Wrong.

"Yes, we are!" Again, Holly and Maddie spoke in unison.

They did this all the time quite unselfconsciously, and Joe was used to it. Didn't even hear it, half the time. Grandmotherly women thought it was "adorable," but when it came to things like begging for riding lessons, it just doubled their pester power. In his darker moments, Joe considered identical twins to be a whole lot less cute than they were cracked up to be…and still he loved these two with every particle in his soul.

"Okay, they are hungry," he said. "There's a bag of potato smiles in the freezer. Put half of them in the toaster oven. Girls, if Grandad doesn't hear the oven timer when it goes off, you tell him, okay? Don't try to get them out of the hot oven yourselves."

He knew they would, if he didn't specifically forbid it. They were incredibly ambitious when it came to attempting practical tasks that they weren't ready for yet. He'd caught them trying to fry their own eggs when they were two.

Dad, Holly and Maddie left again, and Joe found himself wondering just how quickly he could arrange to get the loaner car to Mary Jane, assuming she wanted it, because he really didn't want to leave Dad on his own with the girls for much longer.

## Chapter Two

"A loaner car?" Mary Jane said blankly.

She was still digesting the news that her mangy, neglected kitten of a car had a lot more wrong with it than just a splinter in its paw, and wouldn't be ready until Friday.

"Yes, Dad has a nice little compact, very similar to yours, that he lends to long-term clients if their car is going to be in the shop for a while," Joe Capelli said, in the voice that had been too deep and gruff and husky for singing "Mari-i-i-aa!" in *West Side Story*.

"Well, yes. I do need it." It was impossible to manage the resort in summer without a car. She was constantly running small errands such as picking up new pool chemicals or buying fresh groceries for the restaurant if their regular delivery orders had fallen short. Last week, she'd had to drive a guest to the hospital emergency room.

"Can I drop it over to you in twenty minutes or so,

then," Joe said, "and you can drop me back home? Is that possible? It works out really well for me if you can."

"You're still living over on North Street?" She had no idea where she'd dredged up this detail from the past, but somehow it was there.

If he was surprised, it didn't show. "That's right, with my dad."

"No problem, then." She was mentally sorting through the staffing implications as she spoke. If Lee hadn't already left to drive up to Jay, where she and her fiancé, Mac, were renting a house, Lee might have stayed on until Mary Jane was back with the loaner car, but her absence wasn't a major issue. Nickie could staff the office, and Piri would be happy to put in another hour or two in the restaurant kitchen, as she wanted all the work she could get. "So twenty minutes, you said?"

"Give or take."

"Great! You know where we are?"

She began to give directions, but he cut in with a quick, "No, it's fine, I know it," and then he was as good as his word, shooting into a parking space in front of the resort office about nineteen minutes after they'd ended the call. The little red car looked way too small for him, as he uncurled himself from the driver's seat, but it would be perfect for Mary Jane. Small, zippy, fuel-efficient.

Nickie was already on the phone in the office, answering a guest's question about extra towels, so Mary Jane hurried out and Joe handed her the keys. He'd taken off the grease-stained overalls and was wearing a pair of well-worn jeans and a T-shirt almost the same as the other one, except a paler blue in color.

And cleaner.

Definitely cleaner.

More worn, too, maybe. Through the fabric, she could glimpse the darker patch where he had hair on his chest.

He'd scrubbed his hands and arms and neck and face, she could tell, because his hairline still looked a little damp and she could smell the clean, floral scent of soap. There was even a streak of it on his neck, just below his ear. She had a ridiculous urge to grab a tissue and wipe it off.

"Oh, you can drive till we get to your place, if you want," she said to him. She tried to hand the keys back, but he wouldn't take them.

"Best if you get some practice while I'm still with you, in case it drives a little different than yours."

"Okay, that makes sense, but I'm sure I'll be fine."

Famous last words.

On the passenger side, he seemed even more crowded than he'd been at the wheel, and he had the seat pushed right back. She was distracted by his beautifully sculpted bulk, by the fact that he didn't bother with small talk and by the mental shopping list she was currently creating because the fridge in her apartment above the office didn't have much in it right now. She just hadn't had time to think about grocery shopping the past few days.

Lee was down here working at Spruce Bay only four days a week, which was already too many hours for a pregnant fiancée to be apart from her husband-to-be. Lee and Mac had a small wedding planned for late July, then she would be finishing up at the end of the Labor Day weekend in early September, ready for the birth. Mary Jane was thinking of suggesting that she stop before then.

*I could hire on someone who wants six or seven days a week.*

As a couple, Lee and Mac seemed incredibly happy together, but their relationship had gone from zero to sixty in about fourteen seconds, if you wanted to stick to the automotive theme. She'd gotten pregnant so early into their involvement, they'd had a lot to deal with and sort out in the months since, and they still had decisions to make about where they would settle, long-term. Mary Jane had berated herself more than once for feeling impatient about it.

*Decide, already, so I know where I stand with running the resort.*

*Okay, no, it's not fair of me to think that way. It's not about me. It's about them.*

But sometimes she had the unhappy feeling that nothing was *ever* about her…

"Here," Joe Capelli suddenly said.

"What? Oh, sorry." She'd been barreling down North Street, forgetting that she should be slowing down for him to point out his house. Now she had to brake too hard, and with a garage mechanic sitting beside her, she was self-conscious about her less-than-exemplary driving. "Which one?"

"This one, on the right."

"Oh, wow, it's beautiful!"

"Thanks," he drawled, and she realized that her frankly expressed surprise hadn't been especially complimentary.

She'd driven past this house numerous times before, but hadn't known it was the Capelli family's place. It was a classic white two-story clapboard with dark green shutters, modest in size but impeccably maintained, with a wraparound veranda floored in hardwood, and a shady, grassy garden all around it. At this time of year, the flower beds were full of color and the trees were beautifully green. It was gorgeous.

Now she managed to slow just in time to turn into the driveway, which consisted of two long strips of brick paving with grass in between and on either side. Because she'd turned just a fraction too late and too crooked, Mary Jane missed the strips and drove onto the grass instead, and unfortunately the brick was at a slightly higher level, so when she tried to steer the wheels back onto the harder strips, she could hear the tires scraping before they bumped into place.

She was sweating at this point. Driving badly, after neglecting her own car. Making transparently snobbish assumptions about what his house would be like, when, if he remembered her from high school at all, he would have remembered that she'd never spoken to him or smiled at him and had glared at him or looked the other way with a frozen expression on her face whenever they chanced to meet. He would be in no doubt about what she'd thought of him then, and what she thought of him now.

"Thanks so much for the loan of the car," she said. "Sorry I'm driving it so badly."

"You're doing fine." More famous last words. "I'll let you know when yours is ready. Here's my card, though, in case you want to call and check on how it's going."

He didn't seem keen to linger. Well, why would he be? A quick, "See you, then," and he was out of the car and striding toward the house, his legs looking lean and fit and strong in those faded old jeans, and his butt lovingly sculpted by the soft weave of the—

*Stop it, Mary Jane!*

Before he reached the front porch, she reversed back down the drive and turned into the street, hoping he hadn't noticed that she'd bumped one wheel down off the curb.

Or that she'd been looking at his backside.

Supermarket. What was that list, again? Butter, milk, bread, eggs, cheese, salad, maybe some pasta and a jar of sauce, or steak and vegetables for an Asian stir-fry. Did she have any rice? And Daisy had given her a list for the restaurant, too. She tried to remember the conversation.

"We're out of…" Blank.

*Think, Mary Jane!* She hit the highway and sped up. Joe had been right. This car was so similar to hers, she really didn't have to think too much about it.

So she thought about Daisy's list instead, about Daisy ticking things off on her fingers. But the memory wouldn't come. Cream and— There were two more things. Two items probably with a short shelf life, because they sometimes did tend to run out of those between regular deliveries from their suppliers. Cream and—

Not cheese. Not milk.

She took the exit and there was a red light ahead. It turned green and she thought, "Good, don't have to stop," but the car that was already stopped at the light took longer to get going than she expected. The driver was on his phone and hadn't seen that the light was green, and when he did, he tried to shoot off too fast and stalled. The light turned orange, the driver gave up trying to get through and sat there. Before Mary Jane knew what was happening…

*Crash!* There came the sickening metallic crunching sound of Capelli Auto's loaner car rear-ending the car in front so that it pushed several feet into the intersection. The light turned red, leaving both of them stranded, with horns sounding and drivers steering around them. Mary Jane was shaking like a leaf when she climbed out of the vehicle.

The whole front was badly crumpled. The man in the other car was furious, even though his vehicle appeared to have much less damage. Thank heaven neither of them seemed to be hurt. He wanted her contact details for the insurance, and in a shaky hand she wrote them down on a piece of paper in her purse that, if she'd been more organized today, could have had a shopping list on it and she might have avoided all this.

Because she knew it was totally her own fault.

She was distracted, and she was driving a car that might have been very similar to her own, but wasn't exactly the same. She should have been more careful and alert. The brake pedal took a little longer to grab than it did on her own vehicle, and she should already have known that because she'd slammed her foot on it in front of Joe's house.

People had stopped to help, and someone must have called the traffic police because she saw a vehicle with flashing lights pull up. The whole process seemed to take quite a long time, and when the officers directed her to move the car off the road, she couldn't get it to start. They had to push it onto the verge.

"You'll have to get it towed, and have someone come pick you up. Is there someone you can call?" an officer said.

"Yes, there is."

Unfortunately.

The girls were in the bath when the phone rang. Joe left them alone long enough to grab it, heading back with it toward the bathroom before he'd even figured out who was calling. Even now that they were seven, he never liked leaving them in the bath too long without supervision, and usually found a task to do in his adjacent bedroom while they were in there—laundry folding or internet banking on his laptop.

"Joe?" The voice was female and very wobbly, the reception not that clear, and for one horrible moment he thought it was the girls' mother. That was the only way he ever thought of her, now. Factual. Practical. The woman who'd given them life, but nothing more. Nothing good, anyhow.

It wasn't her.

"Joe, it's Mary Jane Cherry."

"What's up?"

"I've— Something terrible has happened. I'm so sorry. I've crashed the car."

"You've—"

"Rear-ended someone. It's all crumpled in front and it won't start, and it's going to be towed, and I thought you might want it towed back to the garage, and that you might have a towing company you could recommend." She sounded very, very shaken, and undeserving of his immediate inner rage.

*You are kidding me! This is the last thing I need.*

"Wait, are you okay?" he asked.

"I'm fine. I think. Shaken. The police have cited me and I know it was my fault."

"Don't worry. It's insured."

"Yes, I was sure it would be, but still, I am so, so sorry. I'll cover your deductible, obviously."

"Don't worry about that now." He swallowed his anger, told himself that this was going to be way more of a pain in the butt for her than for him, and that these things happened to the best of people on a bad day. "Let me give you the name of a towing company, and yes, have them bring it back to the garage. Do you have a ride home?"

"N-no, I don't." Now she sounded close to tears, but two seconds later she'd brisked herself up, with an effort he could hear over the phone line. "But I'll get a cab, so that's fine."

"I'll come pick you up."

"You don't have to do that."

"I want to see the car."

"Right. Of course."

"Tell me where you are."

She told him and he didn't need to write it down. Pretty easy. He used that supermarket all the time, and knew the traffic lights you went through off of the interstate, just before you got there.

"Five minutes," he promised.

"Thank you so much!"

"Girls, time to get out," he said, when he'd ended the call.

They protested, of course. They were swimming their plastic ponies in there. Apparently there were these newly invented magical creatures called water ponies that could jump like flying fish. As a result, an astonishingly large percentage of the bathwater was now pooling on the bathroom floor.

"No, you really have to come out," he insisted, using the voice they knew meant business. "This minute."

Dad was snoozing on the couch downstairs, and Joe wasn't going to disturb him to ask him to supervise a bath that had already gone on quite long enough. The girls had wrinkled fingers and toes, and the water was tepid at best.

He wrapped Holly and Maddie in their towels and sent them off to their room to put on their pj's while he let the water out and attempted to use a towel to soak up the spills. He might have done better with a mop and a bucket. In their doorway, he told them, "I have to go rescue someone from a fender bender."

"What's a fender bender?" they wanted to know at once.

"A car crash where the cars are damaged but no one's hurt. But she's a little upset, so I can't keep her waiting. You had those potato smiles so you can't be hungry—"

"We are!"

"Well, you can wait, anyhow. I'll be as quick as I can. You play in here and don't disturb Grandad, okay? Unless it's an emergency."

"What kind of emergency?"

"Fire or bleeding. And don't you dare do anything to make either of those things happen!"

Shoot, should he wake Dad up? He was spooky and overprotective about this stuff and he knew it—knew the reasons for it, too. He was trying to let go a little, trying to tell himself that they didn't get themselves into trouble nearly as often as it seemed. They were seven, and bright, and good, mostly…and in no danger. The impulsiveness and lack of any sense of risk had gotten a lot better, the past year or so. And if they screamed for any reason, Dad would wake up. He was sixty-five, not eighty-five, and he was just a little tired.

"Tell Grandad where I've gone, okay, and that I'll be back soon."

"But you said not to wake him up."

"Tell him *if* he wakes up."

Why did these simple conversations always take so long, and involve all these left-field questions he hadn't expected? After a little more back and forth, he got himself out of the house and across to the old-fashioned detached wooden garage, with its wooden doors.

No remote-control opener for this old friend. It contained his minivan, still warm from a day spent sitting in the sun in parking lots at the lake, mini golf and the ice cream parlor, while Dad's pickup was parked in the yard, relegated to the open air. Dad had insisted on that, claiming that the minivan was the more important vehicle, since it was the one that mostly transported the girls. Joe wasn't going to argue with that.

He pushed the creaky old garage doors open, reversed the minivan out and climbed out of it again to go shut the doors because Dad had tools in there that were older than the Declaration of Independence and more precious to him than gold, so they couldn't be left unprotected.

He'd already taken quite a bit longer than five minutes before he even got on the road.

## Chapter Three

What if he didn't come?

Joe had said, "Five minutes," and because he'd been so accurate in his time estimate when he'd picked her up at Spruce Bay, Mary Jane had pinned herself completely on that five minutes and was getting very jittery about the fact that he wasn't yet here.

It had been fifteen minutes at least since she'd spoken to him. The tow truck had come, loaded up the Capelli Auto car and gone again. The helpful witnesses had been interviewed and had left. The driver she'd crashed into, whose car had started on the first try, was long gone, and even the police officers had driven off now.

At least this was June, so it was still broad daylight even though it was now past six o'clock in the evening. But the sky had clouded over and there was a breeze, so it wasn't that warm anymore. Goose bumps had risen on her bare arms and she was starting to shiver—whether it was just from cold or from delayed shock, as well, she wasn't sure.

She felt like an abandoned waif, standing here on the verge while cars drove back and forth through the unlucky intersection, ignoring her. She had begun to think about calling a taxi after all—thank goodness she'd remembered to retrieve her purse from the car before it was towed, so she had money and her phone—when at last she saw a minivan slowing down as it came toward her, and when she peered at the driver she saw it was Joe.

Hang on, was it?

Yes, it really was—Joe Capelli, driving a maroon mini-van, and a rather elderly looking one, at that. "Hop in, stranger," he drawled at her, leaning across to open the passenger door. "Sorry I took longer than I said."

"It's f-fine. I couldn't expect you just to drop everything."

"Well, I did, but dropping everything can still take a while, at my place."

"Oh, o-k-kay." She should probably ask him what he meant by that, but she was struggling so hard not to show that she was shaking. Her head felt as if it had an iron band of pain around it, she hadn't eaten since a pear and a banana for lunch at around noon and her empty stomach felt queasy from shock and cold and sheer misery.

"You're freezing." He quickly reached to switch the air-conditioning off and turn the heating on instead, while all she could do was nod. "I'm sorry, I should have thought of that. The car was warm from the sun, and I was warm from the house. Didn't realize it had gotten so chilly out."

"I'll soon warm up."

He didn't mention dropping her home, and from the route he took, she realized he was going directly to the garage. Maybe she could grab a glass of water there, so she could swallow a couple of the painkillers she had in her purse. When this kind of a tension headache started, Mary Jane knew from experience that it would end badly if she couldn't get those painkillers down pretty soon.

The tow truck was parked out front, the driver in the process of unloading the car. It looked terrible. Who would have thought a low-speed collision at a traffic light could have done so much damage?

"I'm so sorry," Mary Jane said again, the headache making her queasier by the minute.

"The car's at least eight years old. Please don't worry about it."

"Is there somewhere I can get a drink of water?"

"Watercooler in the office. You have a headache," he correctly guessed.

"Yes."

"Got pills?"

"Just need the water."

"I'll get it for you. Stay put." He hopped out of the minivan and went to talk to the tow-truck driver, and she was feeling so bad by this time that she didn't even look, just bent forward, then kept very still and tried to breathe slow and even—in through her nose, out through her mouth—focusing on a single object.

In this case, a pink plastic pony on the minivan's gray-carpeted floor.

Joe Capelli was a family man.

Even in her shaken and fuzzy state, Mary Jane could work that out.

She felt even worse about what had happened, thinking of him arriving back late for his home-cooked meal after this unwanted errand, and disappointing his apron-clad wife and their no doubt adorable brood of brown-eyed children.

Not actually quite sure where the apron was coming from. She couldn't imagine any wife of "Cap" Capelli's ever wearing such a thing.

He came back with a plastic cup of water and she moved carefully to get the pills out of her purse. "Are you sure it's not whiplash?" he said, after she'd swallowed the pills and the water.

"Tension headache," she said. "I get them…when I'm tense."

"Right." He climbed back into the vehicle and she heard the tow truck pulling out into the street.

"Is everything okay?" she asked.

"For today. Listen, do you have someone to take care of you when you get home?"

She didn't answer right away, looking for the best way to admit that she would be spending the evening on her own, either in the office itself or for brief intervals upstairs in a largely food-free apartment, listening for the bell or the phone down in the office, until she closed it up at nine-thirty.

Daisy and her staff would be too busy in the restaurant to take care of anyone but the dinner crowd, and Nickie would leave as soon as Mary Jane was back. Nickie was eighteen years old, bright and perky, efficient enough in her various tasks around the resort but not exactly a nurturing personality.

"Not really," seemed to sum all of this up pretty well.

"Are you hungry?" he asked.

"I think that's part of what's making this headache so bad," she admitted.

"Let me bring you back to my place and feed you, and by then hopefully your head will be better and we can work out what we're going to do about transport for you till Friday."

"It's not your problem, Joe. Surely I've already given you enough grief."

"We'll work something out," he said, quiet but firm, and she couldn't find the words to argue any more. "Toss that cup in the back, if you want," he added. "It's messy enough in there already."

But she couldn't bring herself to do something that untidy when he was being so good, so she held on to it.

North Street was only a few minutes away. She closed her eyes for the drive, and didn't open them until she felt him turn onto those brick strips she'd missed before. He parked in front of a detached garage, then turned to look at her. "Any better?"

"Not yet."

"My girls might be a little noisy for you in the house. Do you want to just sit here in the minivan until the pills kick in? Come in when you're ready. And if there's something you'd like me to bring out to you now, just say."

"No, it's fine. But I will stay in the car. Thanks."

"Juice box? Snack pack of crackers?"

"No, really."

"Okay, then. Front door'll be open, when you're ready. Don't knock, or anything. Just come in." He closed the minivan door almost silently, and she appreciated his concern for her pounding head.

Seconds later, he'd headed for the house and she was on her own, in his minivan, in front of his garage.

*The girls,* he'd said. Two or more. Could be teenagers or three-year-olds, although the plastic pony did suggest the lower end of the age spectrum.

Well, she'd find out soon.

She sat, doing more of the careful breathing, trying to relax her shoulders and neck, and wondering if he could be right about the whiplash. She very much hoped not. After twenty minutes, she felt the pain letting go and the nausea subsiding, and knew it was time to go inside.

"Do you want creamy sauce, or red sauce?" Joe asked the girls.

They did their silent exchange of opinion, seeming to know from just looking at each other what they were going to choose and then announcing it in unison as usual, "Creamy!"

He hoped Mary Jane would approve. He'd thrown a couple of loaves of foil-wrapped store-bought garlic bread into the oven, grabbed a bag of cheese ravioli from the freezer, and dumped premixed and prewashed salad greens into a bowl. The girls loved cheese ravioli, and would happily have eaten it three times a week.

Well, sometimes they did.

It was an easy dinner choice for a busy man, when paired with a container of pasta sauce from the supermarket deli section, and he told himself it was a pretty healthy meal if he made a salad on the side. He just hoped there would be enough of it tonight to feed himself, Dad, the girls and Mary Jane.

Here she was.

She came quietly into the kitchen, still looking pretty washed out but a lot better than before. She had beautiful skin, fair and fine-pored. He'd noticed it before, at the garage, and it was even more obvious under the kitchen lights. She'd looked like a ghost when she was in the grip of the headache, but now there was a faint blush of pretty pink color, and her lips looked lush instead of dry. She was pretty. Not beautiful, but sweet and nice-looking in a girl-next-door way. He wouldn't have valued looks like hers ten years ago, but now he knew better.

*Woman*-next-door, though, he revised. She was his own age, thirty-five.

"Pills worked?" he asked.

"Starting to."

He shook some crackers from a packet onto a plate and said, "Maybe those'll help, till dinner's ready. Want a glass of juice, as well?"

"That would be lovely."

"Glasses are up there." He gestured with his chin as he grated Parmesan cheese. Yes, you could buy the stuff already grated, but he didn't have an Italian last name for nothing. "Juice in the refrigerator."

"Is there anything you'd like me to do to help?"

"No, we're good. I'll call the girls. They're supposed to be setting the table. By the time they're done, it'll be ready. Cheese ravioli, with creamy chicken and mushroom sauce."

"Sounds delicious."

"Not homemade," he warned her.

"Oh, I wasn't expecting..." She trailed off. "I know you wouldn't have time for that."

He wondered what she was thinking, and whether he should give her any kind of explanation. He was a single dad, with no mother in the picture. Well, she would work it out. He hated explaining.

She stood awkwardly, and he racked his brain for a way to make her feel more at ease. Saving both of them, Holly and Maddie bounced into the kitchen at that moment in their pony pj's. "Is it ready yet?" Two voices with but a single thought.

"It will be, when you've laid the table. Mary Jane, these are my girls, Holly and Maddie." Making the introduction, he saw them for a moment with a stranger's eyes—a pair of dark-haired, skinny, energetic, big-eyed and heartbreakingly cute little peas in a pod, dressed in pink. "I got them in a two-for-one sale, as you can see."

She laughed, seeming delighted by them, as most people were. The color in her cheeks grew pinker, and she bent and rested her palms on her thighs for a moment, so she could greet them at eye level. They were small for their age. "Hi, Maddie. Hi, Holly. I bet you were a bargain!"

They hadn't been. They'd cost him a fortune in medical and legal costs over the past seven years, and he was still paying off his debts, but of course he wasn't going to tell her that. The girls laughed at the idea that they'd been a bargain in a two-for-one sale, and he wasn't going to tell *them* the truth about what they'd cost him, either.

Not yet.

Not until they were much older.

Not unless they asked.

They did ask, occasionally—a child's version of the question. "Tell us again, Daddy. Why don't we have a mommy?"

"Because she couldn't take care of you."

"Why couldn't she take care of us?"

"Because she just couldn't." *Because she's a drug-addled, unrepentant mess, and her boyfriends are all dangerous. One of them put you in the hospital for a week, Maddie, and there was no way I was ever, ever letting her have either of you back after that.* "And so we decided that I would take care of you on my own."

Well, a series of judges decided. It had taken a while.

"Where is she, our mommy?"

"Far, far away." *In La La Land, and trust me you don't want to go there.*

"Is she sick? Is that why she can't take care of us?" One time when they'd asked, he'd told them she was sick.

"Yes, she's sick," he had said in answer to this question

ever since, because addiction on such a self-destructive level was a kind of sickness, wasn't it?

"Isn't she going to get better?"

"No, my sweethearts. She doesn't want to get better. That's the problem. If she wanted to, things might be different."

"How could she not want to get better?"

This one defeated him, every time.

"We'll have to wait until you're older before I can explain all that, okay? It's too hard to understand when you're seven."

Mary Jane would understand. Mary Jane might be shocked. He wasn't going to tell her.

In the next room, at the dining table, the girls were counting pasta plates. "One for Daddy, one for Grandad, one for the lady." A whispered consultation. They'd forgotten her name.

"Mary Jane," he called out.

"One for Mary Jane," Holly said.

"One for me," said Maddie.

"And one for me," Holly finished.

"I'm sorry, it's going to be very hard for me to tell which one of them is which," Mary Jane said.

"That's okay. It's hard for everyone, until they know them. There's a trick, though. Maddie has a scar right at her hairline, and it makes her parting fall a slightly different way from Holly's."

"I'll try to remember that!"

The ravioli had floated to the surface in its big pot of boiling water, and the pot was bubbling fiercely, about to overflow. He turned down the gas, spooned up a piece of ravioli and held it out for Mary Jane. "Want to see if this is done?"

She smiled a little hesitantly. "Okay, sure." She stepped

up to the spoon, which he held steady and level with her mouth. She blew on it, a strand of hair falling around her face and threatening to get in the way, and he realized this wasn't what you did when you had a near-stranger to dinner, a grown woman of thirty-five, a ripe, pretty woman who'd already drawn your eye. You did *not* hold out a spoon of ravioli and invite her to test it. It was something he did with the girls.

And the girls didn't blow on the spoon with such a full, kissable-looking mouth, shaped by the blowing into such a perfect kissable shape.

He veered his thoughts away from this dangerous observation so fast that if they'd been car tires, you would have heard them screeching.

But then, with insidious intent, the thoughts crept back again, against his will. Out of an old habit that he hadn't fallen into for a while, he found himself assessing her desirability and availability as a bed partner. It was what guys did when they were players, and he'd been a player from his mid-teens until the age of twenty-six.

On both counts, Mary Jane scored a thumbs-up. She wasn't his usual type—if he had a usual type, these days—but, as he'd noted before, she was attractive, in a quiet kind of way. She had a very nice body, trim yet curvy. And he was pretty sure he would be able to get her into bed if he tried, despite all those glaring, frozen looks she used to give him all the time in high school. There was an innocence about her, and something in her eyes. Heat and hunger. Wistfulness.

*Do. Not. Go. There.*

He was *not* looking for a quick hookup, or even a longer-term connection. He wasn't looking for anything. He'd be crazy to, despite his bouts of loneliness. He was way more cautious than he used to be, and way too committed to the girls and their future. He had too much on his plate right now. He didn't want to hurt anyone, or hurt himself, or confuse the girls, or worry Dad.

No. Just no.

"Um, it seems cooked to me," she said.

He took a firmer hold on himself. Mary Jane's mouth rounding itself to blow gently on pasta was just a mouth, not a disaster. "Good. I'll drain it, then. Garlic bread's in the oven, if you want to grab a hot mitt and take it to the table." After the spoon-blowing incident, asking her to help with ferrying the food didn't seem like such a big deal. She'd already helped herself quite cheerfully to juice, as he'd invited her to do. "Girls, call Grandad."

Dad was probably out of the shower and freshly dressed by now. He still showered at around this time every day, even when he wasn't washing off a day of engine grease. Dad's lifelong habits, and Mom's, had driven Joe nuts when he was in his teens. All that routine had seemed so boring.

He'd vowed he would shake this place as soon as he could and head for California, but by the time he'd graduated high school, Mom had gotten ill and her heart would have broken if he'd left. He'd been pretty egotistical and self-absorbed back then, but he had enough good Italian sense of family to override the ego when it came to Mom.

So he'd stayed on. He'd gotten an associate degree in motor maintenance to please his parents, "So you'll have something to fall back on if the acting thing doesn't work out." Although, of course, he'd secretly vowed never to need a fallback plan.

He'd worked with Dad in the garage until a year after Mom's death and then he'd finally gone to make his fortune in Hollywood when he was twenty-two. Dad had still had Joe's three older brothers reasonably close by—Danny an accountant in Albany, John a paramedic in Burlington and Frank a lawyer in New York City.

Thirteen years later, his brothers were still doing those same jobs in those same cities, each of them with a family, and Dad was still showering before dinner, but now the routines and the habits and the settled lives seemed precious and meaningful and good, compared to the seven years of chaos and fear and heartache and anger and relentless work that Joe had just lived through.

If he could build something like this for himself and the girls, he would feel as if he'd struck gold. He'd just spent six years busting his gut to get through a California law degree part-time, while working to support himself and the girls, and he was taking the reputedly grueling New York state bar exam at the end of July. Having barely studied in high school, he now spent more hours at his desk in a single night—every night, after the girls had gone to bed—than he would have in a month twenty years ago.

Life really was a funny thing.

Mary Jane reappeared in the kitchen doorway, having deposited the garlic bread on the dining table as instructed. She stood a little awkwardly, looking as if she was waiting to be given another task, but there was nothing more for her to do. The girls had transported the salad and the grated cheese. Joe had the big blue ceramic pasta bowl in his hands. "Sit," he told his guest. "We're ready to eat."

The word *Mommy* wasn't spoken.

Mary Jane kept waiting for it. Surely she would have to hear it eventually, and the context it came in would answer some questions. So far, nothing.

The girls were absolutely adorable, and she could see the slight difference in Maddie's hairline that Joe had mentioned. She studied it, as well as both girls' faces, to make sure she didn't get them mixed up in the future.

What future, though? This was one evening, not the start of something.

She couldn't quite believe that she was sitting here like this, part of a three-generation family dinner at a cheerful table in a pretty room. She liked it too much, felt it warming the frozen, rusty parts of her heart in a way that she instinctively knew was dangerous.

Before coming into the house, she'd called Daisy to let her know what was happening, and Daisy had said to take her time and not worry about a thing. She could manage fine without the cream and raspberries and cinnamon. They were part of her breakfast plan, and she'd switch the menu around. "Relax!"

So Mary Jane was relaxing. Relaxing too much. Her headache had completely gone. The meal was delicious. Mr. Capelli…Art…was warm and fatherly and comfortable. "More pasta, Mary Jane. Go on, eat!" he'd told her, and he had been incredibly understanding about the disaster with the car, while Joe made the cutest dad.

*I can't believe I'm thinking this.*

*About Joe Capelli!*

He teased his daughters into minding their table manners, with a look in his dark eyes that was a mix of long-suffering and wry humor. Once, after Holly had said something unconsciously funny, he exchanged a glance of shared amusement with Mary Jane across the top of two dark little heads, and she heated up all over, exactly the way she would have done in high school.

*He's gorgeous, he has these darling little girls, and he's smiling at* me!

The girls were adorable and also very chatty. Not to say exhausting. She learned their birthday, the names of the friends they'd left behind in California, the hair color of their former teacher and a whole list of their favorite foods. She discovered that they were working on a novel called *Happy Horse and All His Friends*. She heard that they didn't like dolls or guns.

But they never mentioned their mother, and neither did Art or Joe, and it seemed a little strange. Halfway through the meal, when the girls paused for breath and another mouthful of ravioli, the two men asked her about Spruce Bay. They'd heard about the upgrading of the resort and wanted to know how that was going.

"Everything's done, and we have the whole place up and running at full capacity," she told them.

"So you're filling up, on weekends?" Art asked, sounding hopeful about it.

"We're filling up during the week as well, from now until Labor Day. Very pleased. Our website is really pulling people in. People can see how beautiful and fresh everything is after the remodel. The spa bath and solar heating for the pool has been a big hit. So have the new barbecue area and the expanded deck for the restaurant."

"Hate to see a slow season, up here," Art said. "So bad for the local economy. That's good that the remodel has paid off. Helps all of us."

"I suppose that's true."

Capelli Auto was indirectly as dependent on tourists as Spruce Bay, because if the people who ran the resorts and motels and restaurants weren't making money, then they weren't paying staff, and if staff weren't getting paid then they would put off getting their cars fixed for as long as they could.

Ugh, but she didn't like this train of thought, because it reminded her of her own slackness in ignoring the noise in her car. If she'd had it looked at sooner, she might not have needed the loaner car today, and if she hadn't been driving the loaner car, she might not have rear-ended—

*Change the subject, Mary Jane.*

"Are you starting school here in September, girls?" she asked quickly.

They nodded. "But we're not sure which school yet."

"Bit of research to do, there," Joe came in.

"And how about over the summer? What will you do? I bet you have all sorts of plans."

"Pony camp," they said in unison, at once. She couldn't believe how often they did this—came out with the same phrase, in the same intonation, at exactly the same time.

"Pony camp! Wow, that'll be great fun!"

"Well…" Joe came in again, sounding reluctant this time. "Pony camp is more aspiration than reality, at this stage. I don't know if it's practical."

*"Dadd-yyyy…!"*

"I know. I get it. You've said. You really, really want to go to pony camp. But I don't know what there is, around here. If there even is a pony camp. Maybe you could help me on that a little bit, Mary Jane. You probably need to answer guests' questions on this stuff, right?"

"Yes, all the time."

"So you'd know what's out there. I know there are a couple of trail-riding places, but do they offer day camps?"

"There's one that does, but in all honesty I wouldn't recommend it. I've sent guests there a couple of times and they've come back with complaints." She paused, wondering if she should mention the idea she'd thought of. If she did, she would be creating a connection with Joe and his girls that it might be safer to stay away from. She said it all the same. "There is one place I'm thinking of that might work…"

For more than one reason, she wasn't sure if she was

doing the right thing. Penelope Beresford didn't go in for advertising, but she still somehow managed to run an equestrian facility that was in high demand. She was British, a former Olympic rider and a highly regarded dressage and jumping coach, and had top-level riders coming to her regularly for intensive training. She also gave riding lessons to local people, and put on occasional two-week vacation day camps for children at her own convenience, seeming to fill them purely through word of mouth.

She didn't offer accommodation for humans, just horses, so the visiting top-level riders usually stayed at the nearest vacation resort, which happened to be Spruce Bay. They were always very well looked after there.

Mary Jane had two of them staying in the resort's biggest and best-equipped family-size housekeeping cottage right now, as it happened. They were a husband and wife team of professional eventing riders, they'd brought a whole string of their best horses to Penelope and would be here for a month. They'd also brought their two children, a six-year-old boy and an eight-year-old girl and a nanny.

It was just possible that some kind of informal vacation day camp might be arranged out of all this, and it was also just possible that if Mary Jane pulled strings for Joe, on behalf of his girls, she might not feel quite so indebted to him and his father for the fact that she'd crashed their car today, while to punish her in return, they were giving her dinner.

Already, she felt drawn into their lives. Should she be holding back, instead?

"I'd have to ask a few questions before I'd have any details for you," she said slowly. "Wouldn't want to get your hopes up."

"Already done that, I'm afraid," Joe mouthed at her on

a drawl, because Holly and Maddie were looking at her as if stars shone out of her eyes.

Mary Jane winced, and mouthed back, "Sorry," and they shared another look. His mouth tucked itself in at the corner, and the expression in his eyes was so complicated she couldn't work it out at all but wanted to solve everything for him anyhow. Her self-control seemed to be lying in a melted pool at her feet, and there was no going back now.

She knew she was in serious trouble.

Serious, horrible, embarrassing trouble, in the space of a few hours.

Over "Cap" Capelli from high school, and two adorable seven-year-old girls.

## Chapter Four

Joe dropped her back at Spruce Bay almost immediately after dinner. Mary Jane insisted on that. "I'm sure you have a lot to do, Joe." He hadn't let her help with cleaning up, and she'd had to content herself with rinsing off a few plates and putting them in the dishwasher.

He didn't argue about dropping her home, and on the drive they talked about the car.

Cars.

Hers and the one belonging to Capelli Auto.

"I'm sorry we don't have a second car to offer you," he told her.

"I'm glad you don't, because I wouldn't take it. I'll organize a rental. And I *will* cover the deductible on the insurance."

"We'll talk about that."

"We're talking about it now, and it's decided."

"Well, no, because it's possible you have some bargaining power," he said. "There might be something from you that I want, that I would be more than happy to exchange for the deductible on the insurance."

Was he talking about—

"I mean," he went on very quickly, "the pony camp thing."

So, no. He wasn't talking about her selling him her body. Just to be clear.

*What is wrong with you, Mary Jane?*

As if she didn't already know.

"You gave me the impression that pony camp would be a special deal with the owner, is what I'm saying," Joe explained. "So if you can help me organize that, put in a word, or arrange a meeting, or whatever it takes, then it'll hugely help with the girls this summer, and you certainly won't owe me for the car thing."

"I'll call Penelope tomorrow, and talk to the Richardsons about it, too." She'd told Joe about them, and their kids and nanny.

"And call me as soon as you know if we can work something out?"

"Of course."

"I'm sorry, I'm nagging you about this as much as the girls would, but at the moment Dad and I are running the garage and looking after the girls between us, and I can already see that it's going to be too much for Dad."

"Of course. They're adorable, but full of energy." It sounded inadequate. All she really knew about kids came from the ones who stayed at Spruce Bay. Some of those could be pretty obnoxious, and it was a testament to the yearning in her heart that she still wanted babies, lots of babies, even when she'd seen that they didn't always stay cute for long.

Joe's girls were definitely cute. What was this really

about in her heart? The man or the girls? If they had a mother… If she was only away for a few days, and it was only by chance that she hadn't come up in conversation…

Maybe this man and his family were completely out of bounds, and even if they weren't…

*I'm scaring myself, feeling like this so fast.*

"He'll be stubborn about it if I just try to send them off to some kind of commercial day care," Joe was saying. "He doesn't think that's good enough. But a pony camp would be their dream come true, and after—" He stopped and muttered something under his breath. "You don't need the detail."

"No, it's fine." She would take all the detail he wanted to give her. She would listen with all her heart.

Not good. Very, very bad.

She waited to see if he would say more, and when he didn't, her disappointment was yet another danger signal on a rapidly lengthening list. She wanted to know everything about him, and she wanted to hear it from him, in his dark, husk-and-syrup voice, and that was scary.

Crushy. Desperate. Something to beat herself up over, not to embrace.

They emerged from the tree-lined Spruce Bay entrance drive and reached the parking area in front of the office, where he halted, leaving the engine idling. "Thank you so much for everything today," she told him, deliberately formal. "For the car, and coming to pick me up, and then dinner. If I can arrange the pony thing, it still won't be nearly enough."

*"Fuggedaboutit,"* he said, like a character in a mafia movie, and not for the first time she found herself wondering why he'd never succeeded as an actor, the way he'd once been so sure he would. He had the looks, the voice and more charisma than any woman could possibly want.

"I'll call you about the pony thing as soon as I have some information," she said.

"Great."

"Right. Bye, then."

She was so determined not to linger in the car that she scrambled out of it with embarrassing haste, and he drove off at once, with just one final wave. After he'd disappeared back into the trees, she stood there for too long, feeling dreamy and unsettled and full of longing and absolutely, completely furious with herself.

The furious part was pretty familiar, and she knew how to handle it. When your thoughts kept steering onto a track that you didn't want, you just had to keep busy enough that they went away purely through being crowded out of existence.

She bustled through the office door and found Nickie fiddling with her manicure and talking on her phone, slouched back in the swivel chair with her knees drawn up and bumping the desk. "She *wants* to? Are you *serious?*" she was saying in teenager shriek.

So, not talking to a guest, then.

When she saw Mary Jane, she quickly ended the call and smartened up her body language, as if she thought she was about to get yelled at. It was almost more annoying than if she'd kept on talking to her friend, because it gave the impression that she considered Mary Jane to be a dragon of a boss.

"Busy?" Mary Jane asked lightly.

"Cabin 12 flooded their bathroom, and Room 4 couldn't get their air-conditioning to turn on."

"That's probably because the air-conditioning couldn't work out if it was supposed to be blowing hot air or cold," Mary Jane drawled. The new reverse-cycle appliances installed during the re-fit could do both. Even though it was a little chilly out now, the cabins had been warmed by the sun most of the day. They should have been cozy but not too hot, and certainly not too cold.

"I know, right?" Nickie rolled her eyes and smiled, and Mary Jane didn't feel like such a dragon anymore. "I actually had to *ask* them what they wanted it for, heating or cooling, because the room felt like the perfect temperature to me."

"So you got it going?"

"We set it at seventy-five degrees and it decided to do some heating. When we get some real summer, they'll probably want it set at sixty-two. Do you want me to clock off now?"

"Just stay for another five minutes while I run over to the restaurant and see how they're doing over there. But unless there's been a disaster you should be fine to go after that."

"Thanks." She smiled and looked at the time on her phone. "What time tomorrow?"

"Let's say noon?"

The office phone rang at that moment and Nickie picked it up. "Spruce Bay Resort. This is Nickie speaking. How may I help you?"

Mary Jane went over to check in with Daisy, but service was winding down over there, and everything had gone smoothly. Daisy insisted she wasn't required. With a team of staff who knew what they were doing, by this time, the restaurant ran almost independent of the rest of the resort. "Take a break, Mary Jane."

"How about you?" Mary Jane suggested. "Don't you want to get home to your husband? Put your feet up?"

Daisy dragged some steam-misted blond hair away from her pink cheeks. "I'm good. I'll be out of here in half an hour."

"Don't know where you get your energy."

Daisy grinned. "I'm told I should enjoy it while it lasts, because once the third trimester kicks in I'll never ever have it again in my whole entire life."

"Ooh, who have you been talking to?"

"A very wise woman in the waiting room at the doctor, who's pregnant with number five."

"Wow." Mary Jane ignored the stupid pang of envy and regret that kicked at her stomach the way Daisy's unborn baby would soon start kicking at hers.

*That was going to be me. Expert mom; big, beautiful family; devoted and thoughtful parenting.*

It wouldn't have been every woman's ambition or choice, but it had been hers, and it hadn't happened.

Heading back toward the office after saying good-night to Daisy, she remembered the early days with Alex, twelve years ago, when she'd begun thinking about marriage. She'd been twenty-two years old when they got together, and twenty-three when she'd decided that he was The One.

She had thought that he would propose pretty soon—the relationship had felt serious to her, important and good and what she was looking for—and she would be married at twenty-four. Maybe wait a couple of years, then have a baby at twenty-six or twenty-seven. She would easily fit in six by the time she was in her late thirties. Six seemed like a good number, enough to fill an eight-seater minivan.

She'd seen herself as a mix of earth mother and soccer mom, the kind of mother that other women looked at with respect, with the kind of kids who were happy and well adjusted and passionate about the things they loved.

She'd thought that she would cook and bake, grow her own vegetables, make her home beautiful with hand-crafted pieces and lovingly restored antiques, take her kids to music lessons and sports, read to them every night.

She'd seen wife, mother and homemaker as an important and interesting career that would absorb and fulfill and challenge her at every turn.

"I don't know how you do it with that many!" everyone would have said. And she would have had some wise, earthy reply. "You just have to stay organized and keep your sense of humor." Or, "I picked the right father for them. That was at least half of it."

But of course Alex hadn't been the right father. He hadn't been the right anything.

He hadn't proposed on schedule, and eventually she was the one who'd brought it up. "Alex, do you see us getting married anytime soon?"

He'd told her there was no hurry. Weren't they happy the way they were? They had plenty of time, why not live a little before they got serious? And then he'd distracted her with shared travel plans for a trip to Cancún, which she'd interpreted as a sign of commitment.

A year later, when she'd turned twenty-six and had at one point a few years earlier thought she might already have been a mom by then, she'd tried again. What about kids? Did he want kids?

When the time was right, he'd told her. There was no hurry, was there? She had another seven or eight years before she had to start worrying about her biological clock, right? Why settle down now, when they were having so much fun?

Yes, but she would never be able to fit in six kids if she didn't have the first of them until she was in her mid-thirties! It just wouldn't work!

Of course she hadn't shared this objection with Alex. She didn't want to scare him off with talk of a big family. Maybe they didn't need to have six, she'd decided. Four would do. Or even three, if he really felt strongly about it.

More time had passed. She was approaching thirty and they still weren't formally engaged. Sometimes she'd wondered if he loved her at all, because he would get distant and distracted, but if she challenged him on it and they fought, he would draw her back in with a romantic gesture and an apology. Flowers, jewelry—he'd been very good at all those easy gestures.

But then a month away from her thirtieth birthday, they'd had a huge fight and before it could get to the gesture-and-apology phase, she'd hit him with a point-blank question. Were they getting married, or not?

Not.

She could still remember the words he'd used.

"Let's be honest. It's never really been headed in that direction, has it?" he'd said, all friendly and matter-of-fact about it, acting as if they'd always both been on the same page and she'd never thought it was a serious relationship, either. As if they'd never discussed it, or children, before. But they had! He'd fobbed her off, let her think a whole lot of things that weren't true.

Lied to her.

She'd been so shocked. She'd told him it was over—had thrown the announcement in his face like a bucket of icy water, and then she'd waited for him to come crawling back. Waited six weeks, before she'd realized it wasn't going to happen.

Less than a year later—and maybe this was the thing that had hurt the worst—she heard that he'd married someone else. She could so easily have gone stalkerish at that point, obsessively looking for evidence that Alex and his new bride had begun seeing each other while he was still involved with Mary Jane herself.

But she hadn't done that, and this gave her some pride. She hadn't done anything wrongheaded at all.

Once she'd known the relationship was really over, she'd been very firm with herself about moving on. She traveled twice every year, when Spruce Bay was closed for its off-season breaks. She kept herself fit and active, well-read and well-informed. She looked after her body and her mind. She worked to make Spruce Bay the best place it could be. She kept up her friendships, and a good relationship with her sisters and mother and father, now retired in South Carolina. She lived her life as fully as she could, even though it was totally different from the life she'd wanted and planned.

Nearly five years later, she was over *him* but maybe still not fully over *it*—the sense of deception, the loss of a dream life that had seemed so realistic and possible, the feeling of having wasted more than seven years on someone who was apparently only keeping her in his life because she was convenient until a better prospect came along.

She would be thirty-six in October.

And hunky Joe Capelli had two adorable little girls with no mother in sight.

*Those two things are not connected!*

Back in the office, she sent Nickie home, then sat down at the computer to check email. The phone rang a few minutes later, and she could tell by which light came on that it was from one of the housekeeping cottages. "Hi, Mary Jane, this is Vanessa in Cottage 7. I'm wondering about getting some more towels."

"Sure, Vanessa. Let me bring some across. How many do you need?"

"Um, four?" came the hopeful answer. "Sorry, there's nothing like horses for getting you filthy."

*I could talk to her right now about the pony-camp thing, and then call Joe tonight to tell him the news...*

Once again, she realized how easily she could turn this into something too important, so she strapped on the self-discipline and simply delivered the towels with a few friendly words to Vanessa and Phil. The pony-camp thing could wait until tomorrow.

## Chapter Five

"Did the lady find a pony camp for us?"

"Her name is Mary Jane," Joe reminded his girls.

"Did Mary Jane find a pony camp for us yet?"

"Probably not yet, since it's not even seven o'clock in the morning, and I only dropped her home at eight-thirty last night, and there's not going to be a pony camp at all if you keep nagging me like this."

"We won't nag," Holly and Maddie promised at once, but Joe didn't believe them for a second.

He felt the temptation to nag, himself, because if he couldn't get a pony camp worked out, then he'd have to opt for something else, and fast. Maybe a teenager, looking for child-minding? That was probably the most affordable and flexible option, but Dad didn't want them using paid child care at all.

For now, they just had to get through another day. He told the girls, "This morning you're going to do some school."

"School?" Holly said.

"But it's summer!" Maddie came in.

"It'll be fun school," he promised, improvising. "I'm going to set you some activities, and you're going to sit quietly and do them all morning, while I'm at the garage. Then Grandad's going to bring you over there, and we'll all have a picnic lunch somewhere, then you'll come back here and watch TV—*quietly*—while Grandad has a nap. Okay?"

Apparently it was okay. Now he just had to think of the fun school activities, while he prepared the picnic lunch.

Well, they could finish their novel. The story was approaching a pretty critical point. Happy Horse had lost three of his friends and was neighing as loud as he could to find them.

Joe could commission them to do some drawings to decorate the garage office. They could read a book and do some craft projects inspired by the story. He could set them up with glue and scissors and old magazines for a collage.

He was probably kidding himself to think that this would last all morning, but it should give Dad some kind of a break before he had to step in and take them to the playground or outside to throw a ball around. Maddie and Holly loved being outdoors and being active, and were so tireless about it. He needed to find the right outlet for all that energy.

Joe discovered that he had begun to yearn for pony camp as much as the girls were...

The morning passed in a rough approximation of his plan, and when Dad arrived at the garage with his pair of beloved granddaughters in tow, he didn't look nearly as wrung-out as he had yesterday afternoon. They went and enjoyed their "chicken-salad sandwich and cookie picnic" in the park, and Joe let them run around on the playground equipment and the rocks until he risked getting back late to meet a client who was picking up his car.

Dad and the girls left while he was putting the client's credit card payment through, and as they walked to the minivan, he could hear them pestering to go back to the park on their way home. "Plea-a-a-se, Grandad! We didn't get to go on the swings."

"All right, but only for fifteen minutes, okay?" came a weary male voice. "Grandad needs a rest after that."

With the client there waiting, Joe couldn't rush out and tell the girls to leave their poor grandfather alone because Grandad needed to go home for his rest right *now,* not in a very elastic fifteen minutes. And then the phone rang and it was Mary Jane. He felt insanely relieved to hear her voice.

Relieved, and maybe there were other things in the mix, too.

"I think I have a plan for you," she said. She had a very appealing voice, bright and warm but not too honey-sweet. "I've talked to Vanessa and Phil and their nanny, Lucy, and they like the idea of joining forces with child care and riding. But Penelope wants to meet the girls first."

"When?" With the strength of his relief, the word came out sounding impatient and abrupt, and he would have softened it quite a bit if he could have had a do-over.

"Whenever you want, I think. She said she was free this afternoon, and so am I…or I can easily be. She wants me to bring the three of you. But this afternoon is probably too soon for you to—"

"This afternoon is great!" If he could quickly finish the two cars he still had to work on, and if Dad could come sit in the office to take delivery of Mary Jane's new parts if they showed up, and handle the payments when people came back to collect their vehicles toward the end of the day, he could do this. He could. He just needed another two hours. "What time?" he asked. "Could it be late-ish? Say three-thirty?"

He was rushing her, pushing too hard for the sake of the girls. He could tell by her awkward laugh. "Um, sure. Let's pencil it in for then, and I'll call Penelope and check. How about I only call you back if it doesn't work for her?"

"So if you *don't* call back, I'll pick you up at, what, three-twenty?"

"That would be work fine. And the Richardsons told me to tell you to make sure the girls wear sturdy shoes with covered toes, not sandals, or Penelope'll have a fit, quote unquote."

"Shoes, not sandals, got it."

And the plan must have worked fine at Penelope's end, also, because he didn't hear back, so at just after three, Dad pulled into the garage with two ridiculously overexcited girls wearing sturdy shoes and grins from ear to ear.


Here were Joe and the girls, Mary Jane saw through the resort office window. Joe climbed out of the driver's seat to come in search of her, and the girls leaped out, too, although they really didn't need to. Joe seemed to be telling them to stay in the car, but they hadn't listened.

They were darting around, pointing at the newly landscaped pool and playground area. They were dressed in matching navy blue stretchy leggings and California-themed cotton T-shirts, one showing the Golden Gate Bridge, and the other a stylized Hollywood Boulevard, and they carried Disney-themed daypacks on their backs.

Mary Jane had decided that the sturdy shoes rule applied to herself as well as to the girls, so she wore white athletic shoes below jeans and a pretty blue-and-white peasant-style top, while Joe had changed out of the car mechanic's clothes he'd presumably been wearing earlier—What was

it that Mary Jane found so attractive about those clothes?—
and had put on sand-colored chinos and a button-down
shirt in a bluish sort of pattern, with a black T-shirt partly
visible underneath, at the open neckline.

He looked good. And casually neat. And respectable
in a way that suggested there was a time when he hadn't
been anything like. A little shiver of need ran through her,
and she squashed it like a rotten tomato.

*Don't. Just don't.*

As she went out to meet them, leaving Nickie to staff
the desk and the phone, she couldn't help noticing how well
the four of them matched, in their coordinating blues. She'd
put some makeup and jewelry on, too, which she mostly
didn't manage to do on an ordinary working day, and she
couldn't pretend about her reasons.

She wanted to impress Joe, and make him notice her.

No, it was even more complicated than that.

More complicated, but not any more admirable or ac-
ceptable. Much less so.

She wanted to look like the kind of woman that the cool,
popular girls from high school would have expected him
to date. The kind he *did* date, in fact.

She was ashamed of herself!

*Don't,* she told herself again.

"Hi," he said, with only the sketch of a smile. "We'd
better get going. I'm a little late. Really sorry. It's so hard
to get everything to happen on schedule."

"We'll only be there a few minutes after three-thirty."

"Don't want to create a bad impression."

He was really keen for this pony-camp thing to work,
and he was anxious about it in a way that touched her heart,
no matter how hard she fought the feeling.

Everything she found out about him spoke of how much

he'd changed since high school, and it intrigued her far more than she wanted.

Everyone changed. No great surprise there. It was a long time ago.

But in his case she wanted to know *how* and *when* and *why,* and whether the changes had been reluctant or willing or hard-won. Had life smacked him down? What choices had he made, and which of them were made willingly? She hated being this curious about him, this hungry for detail, but it seemed to happen every moment she was with him, and every time she looked at his girls.

He drove with efficient speed, following her directions away from the lake and up a forest-lined side road that led to Penelope Beresford's open and grassy twenty-acre property, with the girls craning impatiently in the backseat for their first view of ponies.

"When I see my pony, I'm going to go right up and hug him," Holly announced.

"Me, too," said Maddie. "I'm going to go right up and climb on and *ride* my pony."

"I'm going to *jump* on and *gallop* my pony."

"No, you absolutely one hundred percent are *not,*" Joe said. "No hugging, and definitely no jumping on and riding! That's the quickest way to make pony camp never happen."

The fizz level in the backseat dropped a few notches. "Why, Daddy?"

"Because you don't know anything about real ponies, you only know about them from books, and two led pony rides at fairs, and you have to do exactly as you're told until you start to learn. It takes a long time to learn to ride a horse well."

After a moment of thick silence, he added to Mary Jane, with a quick glance in her direction, "I hope this isn't a dumb idea." The glance seemed to link the two of them together, as did the note of appeal in his question. "Are they too little for this? Too willful? Maybe their obsession will disappear the moment they come face-to-face with the reality of piles of poop and getting accidentally trodden on by a hoof in a metal shoe."

"We'll have to let Penelope make that decision. I told her they were seven, and that they didn't have any riding experience."

He gave a sigh of relief at the wheel. "So at least we're not coming here under false pretenses."

"This is the entrance, here on the left." She gestured, and he slowed, and she couldn't help watching his arm on the wheel, bare to the elbow where he'd rolled up his sleeve. It was a gorgeous arm, tanned and hard and lightly covered in dark hair, and she wondered how it would feel if it was wrapped around her, or if she ran her palm down its length.

How would it feel to have those arms reaching out for her as she went toward them? How would it feel to watch him hefting an axe or a hammer? What would he look like soaping himself in the shower? He could do pretty much anything with those arms and those thighs and that hard, flat torso and those strong hands, and she thought she'd like to watch it all.

*Oh, Mary Jane!*

She just couldn't stop herself.

Her only hope was to at least keep her awareness from showing.

He turned off the road and pulled up at the closed gate, bordered by railed wooden fencing painted in white. Mary Jane jumped out to open it, waiting to close it again behind the vehicle after Joe had driven through.

"You're going to have to learn to do the gate, girls," Joe said.

And even this sounded exciting to them. "You always have to leave gates the way you find them," Maddie said knowledgeably. "If they're closed, you never, ever leave them open."

"And stables," Holly added. "You have to leave them clean, every day."

"I've been reading them books for kids on how to take care of horses," Joe said in another aside to Mary Jane, with another glance. "They can't get enough of them."

"So they know the theory, at least!"

"They do. Are you remembering the books, girls?"

Holly parroted a rule. "Never walk behind a horse if he doesn't know you're there, or he might get startled and kick you."

Maddie had another one. "Hold your hand flat when you give them carrots, so they don't accidentally crunch your fingers."

"We don't have any carrots," Joe pointed out.

"Yes, we do! We have a million carrots! Grandad said we could. We put a whole bag of them in our backpacks."

"Of course you did," he muttered, and Mary Jane had to hide a smile. She was enjoying this—and him…and his relationship with his girls—far too much, and there didn't seem to be a thing she could do about it.

"And we have our swimsuits and towels, too, just in case, for later, at the beach or the pool," Holly said. "Grandad says we might have time. He doesn't know how long we'll be out."

Maddie explained, "That's why our backpacks are so heavy."

"I guess Grandad is giving me a hint that he doesn't want you back too soon," Joe muttered.

Mary Jane hid another smile.

Penelope was trotting a horse round a corral on a long rope, but turned at the sound of Joe's car. She spoke to the big, dark, glossy, loose-limbed creature, and it obediently slowed to a supple walk, then turned toward her, came closer and came to a halt.

The girls climbed out of the car with a sudden showing of shyness and caution, which was probably a great relief to Joe, who was watching their every move from behind his sunglasses as if he feared they might attempt a few circus tricks on the first animal they could find.

Penelope called to a young woman working beside the large barn, who went to take over the work with the horse in the corral. At least, Mary Jane assumed it was work.

And that it was a corral.

She was as far outside her area of experience as were Joe and the girls. Penelope let herself out of the fenced round enclosure and came toward them.

"Penelope, this is Joe Capelli and his girls, Holly and Maddie." She gestured carefully, making sure she pointed at the right twin as she said each name. She was proud of herself for being able to tell them apart, which was ridiculous, really. It wasn't exactly a marketable skill. And she knew quite well what it was about. She was showing off to Joe.

"Hello! Isn't this good!" Penelope said, very brisk and British.

"We're twins," Maddie told her. "But my hair is a bit different on my forehead, that's how you tell us apart." She pushed her hair back. "See?" She was unselfconscious about it, but Mary Jane was surprised—shocked, really—at the size of the scar, even though Joe had told her it was there.

He'd been so matter-of-fact about it, mentioning it only

as a way of telling the girls apart, but it would have been dramatic and very visible if Maddie's hair hadn't provided a disguise. He hadn't mentioned the cause of the injury, and this immediately added itself to the growing list of things that Mary Jane shouldn't…really *shouldn't…must not*…be so curious about.

Maddie let the hair flop onto her forehead again, and the scar vanished behind its handy screen.

"Yes, I can see you're twins," Penelope said. "Hello, Maddie. Hello, Holly. And Joe." She held out her hand, after wiping it on the thigh of her jodhpurs. "Sorry, not very clean."

"I'm a car mechanic," Joe said. "So don't worry about it."

"And since you're twins, perhaps I'm going to have to find you two matching ponies," Penelope said.

"But we want different ponies!" Holly protested, loud and serious. "I want a black one, and Maddie wants a gray one. We decided."

"Holly…" Joe began, wincing.

Penelope was unperturbed, staying cheerful and no-nonsense in her manner. "We have a black one, but not a gray. We have some paints. Do you know what those are?"

"Patchy," Maddie said.

"Yes, very pretty patchy markings. To start with, though, you'll have to share the black pony." She took a phone out of her pocket and sent a quick text. "I'm going to give you a lesson, taking turns on our lovely old girl, Suzie. She's a Shetland pony. Laura, one of my working students, will find some riding boots and helmets for you. I'm just calling her in from the back field. We have plenty of different sizes, so something will fit."

"Right now?" both girls said. "A riding lesson?"

"Yes. Don't you want to get started?"

"Yay!" They clapped their hands and jumped up and down.

"Is this really all right?" Joe asked Penelope. "I'd expected we'd mainly be talking about what this involved, today."

"I just like to have a little look at them before either of us commits ourselves to anything," Penelope said very firmly.

"They've never ridden before. Well, a couple of led pony rides at fairs."

"That's all right. It'll still be good to have a look." She smiled, and Mary Jane had the strong sense that she knew exactly what she was doing.

It took fifteen minutes to get both girls kitted out in the right boots and helmets, stored in a big and very neatly arranged tack room attached to the main barn. Mary Jane expected to find Suzie, the Shetland pony, already saddled and waiting, but apparently she was still in her day yard and had to be caught and groomed.

Penelope took the girls with her "to help," asking Mary Jane and Joe to wait by the round corral where the big horse had now finished his workout and was being led away. It was strange to be standing here with him like this, looking like a couple. If anyone else had been around, that was what they would have thought—that she and Joe were two ordinary parents, of two very cute little girls. They must look as natural together as the perfect family in a commercial on TV.

Mary Jane's heart kicked.

She *wanted* that. She'd always wanted it. Confidently, then angrily, then miserably, then desperately.

She couldn't possibly want it with Joe already, because she barely knew him. High school didn't count. Knowing his father didn't count.

But she wanted it in the abstract, she'd wanted it for so long, and she was scared by the thought of how easy it would be to graft her painfully longed-for fantasy onto this gorgeous man and his adorable daughters.

It would be wrong to do that. A disaster. Joe and Maddie and Holly weren't a fantasy come to life. They were real people. Complex. Flawed.

And so was Mary Jane.

Very, very flawed, she felt right now.

Joe shifted his weight, looked around, scuffed at the dirt. He was ridiculously good-looking in this setting, dark glasses resting their lower rims against his perfect cheekbones, his body strong and beautifully molded beneath the shirt, his dark hair threaded with tiny silver and golden glints in the summer sun and his naturally olive skin smooth and healthy. But he was as tense as a cat on hot bricks, and when she put aside her own issues, Mary Jane could feel his tension like a writhing snake in her own stomach.

"What are you nervous about, Joe?" she had to ask.

"That they'll fail."

"Is this a test?"

"Ohh, you know it is!" He shook his head and whistled. "And Penelope's right. She can't make a promise to us about this camp idea if they're going to be brats."

"They're not brats!"

"They can be." He thought for a moment. "Not brats. Just kids. Too much energy. Too much will of their own. Too young to understand, sometimes, that rules are there for a reason."

"You're afraid they really will just jump on the pony before they're told?"

"Yeah," he said simply. "That, or worse. Their mother

had no impulse control whatsoever. If I ever see her personality coming out in them…" He stopped.

It was the first time he'd ever mentioned the girls' mother, and he was saying it in the past tense. "Had" not "has." What did that mean?

"You get scared about genes, sometimes," he added.

He leaned his folded arms on the top railing of the corral, with one boot-clad foot propped on the bottom rail, and scowled at the big circle of dirt in front of him. Mary Jane was intensely conscious of every line of him, every movement he made. The shape of him seemed to change her own body. When he leaned, she shifted. When he sighed, she took in a huge breath.

"I guess you do," she replied, hearing how inadequate it sounded. She leaned on the rail, too, but sideways, half facing him, with one arm spread along the sun-warmed wood, unable to stop herself from looking at him. When she touched the wood, it half felt like touching his skin— silky, hot, hard.

There was a silence, and still no sign of the girls, Penelope or the pony.

"She's a mess," Joe said suddenly. "That's why I have full custody."

"Oh, I'm so sorry." Hmm. Instantly flustered, she added quickly, "I mean, that she's a mess. Not sorry that you have—"

"It's okay." He glanced at her, making her aware of how close they were standing. "I knew that's what you meant. You were probably wondering, last night at dinner. Not exactly the classic nuclear family."

"I was," she admitted.

"You need to know some of this, I've realized. But I never know how to bring it up with people."

"Well, it's not anyone's business."

"You're helping me with this camp thing, you do need to know. In case something comes up. Behavioral issues. They had a rough few years before they came to me, and I had to fight pretty hard for them."

"Fight?"

"For their safety. To have them with me. They're great now, mostly, but occasionally there are some signs. Nightmares, or moments when they just lose it. And when they get really excited and willful… Yeah, I do get scared."

Which was the cue for one seven-year-old in a riding helmet to appear around the corner of the barn, leading a shaggy black pony roughly the size of a large but very well-fed dog, walking very steadily and carefully and seriously, while her twin was walking a few yards behind them, grinning from ear to ear. Penelope was on the opposite side of the pony, Suzie, walking right beside the shaggy head, keeping an eagle eye on the proceedings.

Right now, it didn't look as if Joe had anything to fear.

Holly was the one grinning. Mary Jane could tell once they'd come closer, even though Maddie's hairline was hidden under the riding helmet now.

*Well, huh,* she thought. *I can tell them apart without the clue!*

It seemed like a triumphant achievement, and she wanted to show it off to Joe, even though she didn't know quite how she was managing to do it, the differences were so subtle. Still, she was sure. Maddie was the twin leading the horse, Holly was walking behind.

"I had my turn leading her before," Holly explained. "Now Maddie's having her turn."

"I can see that," Joe said.

"We're doing it exactly right, Penelope says."

"Are you supposed to be calling her Penelope?"

"Yes, they are." Penelope smiled. "I told them that was

what I wanted to be called. First names are just as polite as Mr. and Mrs., as long as they're used respectfully." It was quite clear that Penelope intended to be spoken to respectfully. She turned to the girls. "Right, now I'm going to open the gate into the round pen, and we'll tie Suzie to the rail inside it while we groom and saddle her. You can help me bring the grooming kit and her tack from the tack room."

*"Yes!"* the girls said. They clearly wanted to hop up and down again, but Penelope must have told them that sudden movements would startle the pony, because they kept their hopping in check, and in general seemed a whole lot calmer and more in awe of the experience than they had been earlier.

Penelope tied the pony's lead rope to a piece of twine, and said, "Do you know why we use the twine, girls, instead of tying the rope directly to the rail?"

"No..." They sounded disappointed in themselves. Joe was watching and listening so intently that Mary Jane feared he was forgetting to breathe. She began to forget to breathe herself.

"So that if Suzie gets a scare and pulls away, she'll just break the twine instead of hurting herself fighting the strong rope, or breaking the yard."

"Could she really break the yard?" Joe asked.

"Well, this one couldn't, but my big warm-bloods and Thoroughbreds could do some damage to themselves or the rails, especially my stallion, if they were really fighting to get loose and couldn't."

"Don't some of them work out how easy it is to break the twine and get free?"

"Occasionally. Some of them learn to untie the knot in the lead rope, instead! Mostly they're happy to stand like this, and happy to be caught from their fields. When they're well-trained, they like the riding partnership with humans, and they like being groomed. They definitely like the food! Come along, girls. I have things for you to carry."

The three of them disappeared again, back to the tack room.

"I should probably tell you more about their mother," Joe said as soon as they'd gone. He did another one of his restless shifts, swapping his feet on the bottom rail of the yard, and turning slightly to face her.

They were standing too close. Too close for Mary Jane, anyhow. She knew it…felt it…could almost feel his body heat…but didn't want to move away in case he thought—

Well, fill in the blank.

In case he thought she was uncomfortable with him, or *not* uncomfortable with him. In case he realized that what she really wanted was to get much, much closer.

"Don't, if you're not comfortable about it," she told him.

"Look, of course I'm not comfortable, it's not a good story, but you might need to spell it out a little more to Penelope, or to the parents of those other kids, if they're all playing and riding together. I don't want to just dump it on them, but they're staying at the resort, and you've known Penelope for a while. It'd be better coming from you, when you can pick the right moment. Someone besides me and Dad needs to know about this."

"Then of course, tell me."

"They were abused when they were little. One of their mother's drug-addled boyfriends. It was going on for a while before I knew. And then even after I knew, it took a while before I could get them permanently away from the situation."

"That must have been horrible!"

"Yeah." He was silent for a moment, clearly looking for what to say next. "That's how Maddie got the scar," he continued eventually. "Holly's not scarred, but hell, she was bruised. And their mother wasn't any better than the boyfriend. Was worse, in her own way." He shook his head. "Chronic neglect. Raw bottoms from diaper rash because she left the same one on for so long. She gave them soda in their baby bottles, instead of formula or milk, if she'd run out. Do you have any idea what that much sugar in a bottle does to their teeth?"

"I can imagine."

"They had cavities in their baby teeth before they were two. I got custody as soon as I could, but she still had some rights, and the court gave her more access than I wanted, for a while." He made a frustrated sound. "I'm probably not telling any of this in the right order, or the right way. Sheesh, details about their teeth!"

"They paint a picture, Joe. Women love details, don't you know that?" She gave him a sidelong grin and he grinned back, which made her regret the moment of flirtation at once.

And they'd run out of time. Penelope and the girls were coming back—Holly carrying the handle of a black plastic carrier that looked like an open toolbox, Maddie carrying a padded saddlecloth and a bridle and Penelope holding the saddle. She rested it on the middle rail of the corral— or, no, round pen—then took the saddlecloth and bridle from Maddie and laid them on top.

"Can we find a time?" Joe said quietly to Mary Jane. He looked at her with those eyes, and they were suffering and serious again, yet they were the same eyes he'd flirted with back in high school. Flirted with just a moment ago. "To talk, I mean? I want to do this properly, not in snatches. Privately."

"Of course."

"Maybe after this? When I drop you back? Could the

girls have a play down by the lake, or a swim in the pool, and we can watch them and talk?"

"Yes, that's fine. Of course," she repeated.

"We could swing by a coffee shop on the way through and get a latte, or whatever you like to drink."

"You don't have to do that."

"Least I can do is buy you a coffee, since I'm taking your time."

"I broke your car," she reminded him.

"Yeah, you did." He grinned again, suddenly, and her stomach kicked and dropped and her limbs went funny. What was she, fourteen? "You are going to be very, very sorry about how much I'm going to milk that."

She wasn't going to be sorry at all, Mary Jane knew. She was going to be painfully, embarrassingly glad.

They both watched while Penelope showed the girls how to groom the pony, clean the dirt out of her hooves and put on the saddlecloth, saddle and bridle.

"She's so little!" Holly said.

"Is she going to get any bigger?" Maddie asked.

"No, this is as big as she'll ever be. She's not a baby horse. She's a grownup pony. Actually she's quite an old girl. She's twenty." Penelope looked across at Joe and Mary Jane. "And very tolerant." Her blue eyes were twinkling. "Now, which of you is going to ride first, I wonder?"

"Holly," said Maddie quickly.

"Is that all right with you, Holly?"

"Yes, I *want* to go first!" Mary Jane had started to realize that Holly was often the one to take the lead, while Maddie was just that little bit more cautious.

Penelope showed Holly how to mount by putting her booted foot in the stirrup and then swinging her leg over. She arrived in a seated position in the saddle wearing a big smile, while Suzie simply stood there, steady as a rock.

It was a lovely lesson. Mary Jane could feel Joe start to relax as each twin in turn listened very seriously to Penelope's instructions and was clearly trying her very hardest to do everything exactly right. There was no jumping on and galloping, no silliness, no questioning of anything Penelope said.

The older woman let the pony around the circular pen for most of the lesson, but both girls had a few minutes of riding on their own at a walk, and were able to use the reins and their legs to change direction in the middle of the round pen and go back the other way.

"Next time, we'll trot," Penelope said.

Beside Mary Jane, Joe let out a carefully controlled breath. "Next time," he murmured. "So I guess that means they've passed."

"I would have passed them," Mary Jane said. "They've been adorable."

She found it hard to drag her eyes away—from the girls themselves and from the sight of Joe watching them. The grins on the girls' faces, or the very serious moments when they tried their hardest to do exactly what Penelope was telling them. "Heels down. Sit deep in the saddle and tall in your back." How cute was a seven-year-old trying to concentrate that hard!

And as for Joe…

His eyes lit up every time they earned Penelope's praise, and he watched intently every time they were asked to do something new. When they beamed at him and said, "Look, Daddy!" he beamed back and said, "Yes, I can see!"

He hadn't brought a camera with him and didn't get out his phone to take pictures, either, and Mary Jane liked that, too—that he was just here, in the moment, focusing on the girls not on obsessively capturing their every move. She'd noticed that with some of the resort guests sometimes, especially the men. They were so busy bagging the prize of endless video and photos, they never truly saw anything while it was actually happening. Joe wasn't like that.

Maddie climbed down from the pony, but the girls weren't quite finished yet. Penelope had them help unsaddle and groom the pony again, then asked them to use a special scoop and brush to clean up the scatter of manure that Suzie had left in the round pen, while Penelope herself led the pony back to her day yard. The girls were thorough about it, Holly saying to Maddie, "You've missed a bit," and Maddie directing Holly to move the scoop closer.

Neither Joe nor Mary Jane missed the way Penelope looked at the state of the round pen when she returned. Had they done a good enough job? Apparently yes. "Good girls," she said, then to Joe, "I'm happy to have them. The Richardsons are here for another three weeks. Mary Jane, you said they're happy to work something out with Lucy's hours and pay?"

"Yes, we didn't get down to exact details, but they thought it would be great for their two to have some other kids to play with, while they're here. I thought we should wait to work everything out until after you'd met them."

"They've been working on a schedule of the kids riding in the mornings with the help of Lucy and one of my working students, while I'm coaching Vanessa and Phil. That takes a while because they've brought eight horses."

"Vanessa and Phil don't ride with their kids?" Joe asked.

"No, we've concluded it's a bit too much like husbands teaching their wives to drive a car. When it comes to formal lessons, Jessica and Simon learn better from someone else, but they do go for trail rides with their parents sometimes and that's lovely and stress-free."

"Maddie and Holly won't be ready for trail rides just yet."

"No, but that's fine. It'll come sooner than you think. At lunchtime, Lucy takes the children on an outing or back to Spruce Bay for swimming and that kind of thing for a few more hours in the afternoon, while Vanessa and Phil finish here. I expect that's how they'll want to continue, if that works for you, Joe."

"Sounds perfect," he said. "Thank you. I really appreciate this. You can't know how much."

"I hate seeing children cooped up inside in front of television and computer screens all day," Penelope said matter-of-factly. "I've seen a love for horses save children's lives. Literally. It's given them a passion and an outlet when otherwise they would have been lost to drugs or crime. And I've seen children with autism or cerebral palsy come to life on horseback, after they've been imprisoned in their own bodies by their disability."

Joe nodded without speaking, and Mary Jane thought that she wasn't the only one who'd sensed him tense up at the mention of drugs and crime. Penelope seemed pretty perceptive. "Thank you," he said again after a moment.

He was quiet in the car as they drove back to Spruce Bay, and so were the girls. As they detoured to Bolton Landing to pick up the coffees Joe had promised, he said to them, "I thought you'd be all chatty about the riding."

"We're thinking."

"About ponies?"

"We're revising our lesson," Holly said.

"So we don't forget how to saddle and groom, next time."

"We're in heaven," Holly added.

"Oh, you are?"

"Yes, it was just so heavenly, Daddy," Maddie said, her sober mood suddenly erupting into excitement again.

"We can't even talk about it, it was so, so amazing and heavenly."

Holly added, pronouncing each word with emphasis, "We are more in love with ponies than ever."

It sounded impossibly solemn and unnatural, and Joe said, "Didn't we read that in a book?"

"Yes, in *Laura Loves Ponies,*" Holly told him.

"In Chapter Four, after she goes for a trail ride with her friends Ella and Gracie and her new pony, Poppy. Don't you remember, Daddy?" Maddie elaborated.

"Remind me."

"She comes back and she's all tired and happy, and the sun is setting in the western sky, in shadings of mauve and lemon and pink and gold, and as Poppy munches contentedly on her oats and hay, the book says Laura is more in love with ponies than ever."

"You're right," Joe said with a straight face. "I do remember that bit."

Mary Jane decided that she knew just how Laura, Maddie and Holly felt about the "being in love" thing. The only problem was, she wasn't sure that the feelings flaring inside her were just for ponies.

## Chapter Six

"You must be wondering what the hell I was doing, letting any of it happen," Joe said. It was a question he'd asked himself a thousand times, looking back. He never felt he really had the answers.

Mary Jane let him off the hook, of course. She sat there in a blue-and-white painted Adirondack chair beside the solar-heated Spruce Bay pool, sipping a latte from a thick paper cup while the girls swam and Joe sat in a matching chair beside her, and she made all the right noises, of course.

Not his fault. Must have done everything he could. Heartbreaking choices. Yada yada.

Mary Jane was too good to him, he decided. Way too nice. Out-of-his-league nice. Nurturing and forgiving and generous and warm. It was a new feeling to be on the receiving end of all that. He'd never dated a nurturing woman before. If you were talking emotional maturity, it was possible he'd never dated a *woman* before. They'd all been silly girls at heart, tricked-up in overly sexualized adult bodies.

"Well, *I* wondered," he said, almost angrily.

She ignored the anger, and just asked quietly, "So how did it happen?"

"The pregnancy was an accident. Obviously."

"I would really like to hear it from the beginning."

When was that? He let out a sigh between his teeth, as he tried to put it all together. "Okay, well, you probably know I wanted to be an actor in high school."

"The whole of high school knew that."

"Ouch!"

"No, no." She looked stricken, sat up straighter and twisted to face him. "I didn't mean it that way." She brushed a strand of hair back from her face with a frown and a distracted gesture, and he saw for the first time how nicely the blue-and-white top clung to her curves, and how pretty her nails were. Almost as pretty as her mouth. They were neat and oval with a professional French manicure, and he had an uncomfortable image flash into his mind— those nails lightly scraping against a man's skin.

His skin.

*Jeesh!*

"No?" he said on a growl, fighting to break away from the pictures in his head.

"Really. I just meant that we all saw you in *West Side Story* and *Phantom of the Opera* and you were fantastic."

"High school productions, and not a big-money high school, either."

"High school productions where you stood out like a sore thumb. I mean, in a good way."

"Glad you added that." No, this wasn't right. He didn't want to talk about high school musicals. And he definitely didn't want to think about her pretty nails and her nice curves. "We're getting distracted."

*I'm getting distracted more.*

"We are."

The girls were happy in the pool, and the sun was still on the blue water, although it was almost six o'clock. There were a couple of other kids in the pool, too, and Holly and Maddie were making friends. Unfortunately, the other kids weren't Jessica and Simon Richardson, so Joe didn't think the friendship had much chance of lasting.

The relationship that the girls would build with the Richardson kids was another unknown factor in all this. What if the girls sabotaged it with difficult behavior? What if Vanessa and Phil decided they were a bad influence? Was he being too paranoid about this?

*Talk about it, Joe. Tell her about why there might be a problem.*

"I was itching to get out to California right after high school," he said to Mary Jane, "but Mom was sick by then and I didn't want to leave. That was when I got the car-mechanic qualifications. Which have come in way more useful than I ever expected." He laughed and heard that it sounded a little bitter, and hated what she might think.

"I heard about your mom," she was saying. Maybe she hadn't caught the bitterness. "I was really sorry."

"Yeah. Thanks. I mean, it's a long time ago, now, but it was rough on Dad. They were good together. After she died, he told me I should go follow my dream. Insisted on it, really, and it was as if I'd been shot out of a cannon. I went to L.A., I worked so hard. Fringe theater, bit parts, extras, walk-ons, wearing sweaty rubber costumes in shopping malls to promote toothpaste and energy drinks. The day I had my first line in a TV commercial, I was walking on air."

She laughed. "What was the line? Do you remember? I'd love to know!"

"That's easy." He was totally distracted by the delight on her face. "Wow."

"Wow? Um… Do you mean…"

His turn to laugh. "Sorry, I mean that was the line. The word, I should say. *Wow.* But it, plus some of the other stuff, was enough to get me a decent agent, and then things almost started to happen."

She made a sympathetic face. "Only almost."

"It's such a tough game."

"Oh, I'm sure!"

"A heck of a lot of people would have killed to get as close as I did." He told her about the audition callbacks for the crime drama, and the other guy getting the role.

"That show is still running!" she said.

"It is. Although he's left it now, and gone on to bigger and better things, as the whole world knows."

"That could have been you."

"Don't let myself think about that too much. Anyhow, that was around the time I met the girls' mother." He couldn't say her name. It was stupid, but he just couldn't. It was Victoria, and he never ever said it out loud, or even thought it, if he could help it.

Some day, Holly and Maddie would want to know, and he guessed he would manage to make it cross his lips at that point, but for now, no thanks. "Part of me wishes that it had never happened."

Mary Jane made another sympathetic noise. Her eyes were really lovely at the moment, all large and shining with empathy, and such a bright clear greenish-blue. She was way too nice. Way too nice for him. Way too nice for what he had to give, and what he would need to ask in return.

*Focus, Joe. Tell her properly. Do her that favor, at least.*

"She was just like me, trying to make it in L.A. She'd done some modeling in New York and I didn't know it at the time but she was deep into drugs there. She was incredibly young when she started her modeling career, sixteen, out of her depth, living away from her family, full of herself. So beautiful. Incredibly, stunningly beautiful."

Mary Jane nodded.

"What some people call black Irish," he told her. "Dark hair and dark eyes and fair skin."

"Like that Irish band, the Corrs."

"In coloring, like the Corrs, very much. She was twenty-two when we met, fresh and stunning, and I was twenty-six."

"How did it happen? That you met, I mean?"

"Oh, pure chance. In a diner. We smiled at each other, started talking. I had no idea. Her parents had stepped in, got her off the drugs, helped her to set herself up on the West Coast so she could switch from modeling to acting. They thought the change would help, and it did for a while. When we met she was clean, but I had no idea about the battle to get to that point, or how easily she would tip back over the line. I thought she was as driven as I was, but it was a different kind of drive. Just a wildness. She was crazy hungry for life. For squeezing every drop out of it, she always said, but her interpretation of that was so destructive. Half the time when she was out—networking, I thought, trying to be seen, going to openings—she was actually scoring and using and partying while the buzz lasted."

He stopped and gathered his breath, hoping he wasn't taking too long over this. He wanted Mary Jane to understand as completely as she could. Why was that? Why did it seem important? She was still listening—she was the kind of woman who listened with her whole soul—but if the girls got bored in the pool, they could easily interrupt.

He kept going. "But the drug use was only intermittent at that point because she was getting auditions, still some modeling. It kept her focused that first year. It gave her a reason to at least try to stay strong. It let me think I knew what was happening in our relationship, even though I didn't at all. Then came the pregnancy."

Mary Jane looked…shocked? Was that it? She said in an odd tone, "She wasn't happy about it?"

He could only be honest. Pointless being anything else. "Neither of us was. It was the last thing we were ready for, especially when we found out it was twins. We went around and around for months, considering our options. I was trying to put money together, trying to get acting work. I thought if either of us could get some kind of a break—a movie or a series—we'd have money pouring in, could do the whole Hollywood nanny thing. We'd look like Brad and Angelina. People would love us." He shook his head. "Sounds naive now. *Was* naive. Anyhow…"

"It didn't happen," Mary Jane filled in gently. He didn't know what she was really thinking, at this point. Maybe she gave everyone this kind of attention when they talked.

"Didn't happen," he repeated. "We had the girls, and it was hard. They were born two months early. They were pretty healthy and strong, only in the hospital for a few days, thank goodness, but when they came home they didn't sleep, they cried all the time for weeks and weeks, we had no money, because the birth and the hospital stay cost so much, and I think their mom was using again within a couple of months of the birth as an escape. She couldn't take her career tanking. That was a huge part of it. She'd been told over and over that she was a star since she was about fourteen, and suddenly there was no one saying that anymore. The addiction problem spiraled down incredibly fast. You have no idea. Or perhaps you do. If you've seen it close up…"

"I haven't. I've led a very sheltered life." His gaze caught for a moment on the ghost of a wry smile, and he sensed some regret, and some self-recrimination.

"You're lucky," he told her bluntly, seeing no need for her to apologize for being sheltered. For being *normal*. "We split up. I didn't really know about the relapse into drug use at that point. Definitely not the extent of it. So again I've been telling this wrong, because you're going to think I let her take the girls when I knew she was using."

*Careful, Joe! Careful what you let her believe…*

"No, I wouldn't—"

"Don't. It's okay. We split up because we were just wrong together, and it turned out the only thing that ever made the relationship work was the fact that we were two beautiful people trying to get famous." He stopped. "You can say *ouch* again, if you want. Two beautiful people trying to get famous. Doesn't that sound great? Doesn't it sound meaningful? It wasn't beautiful. It was ugly."

"Ouch," she answered obediently.

"Thanks," he said, and then he just couldn't stand the honesty in those eyes of hers. The confession came out blunt and abrupt and full of the usual guilt. "It's not true when I said I didn't know she was using after the girls were born. I accused her of it, but she denied it point-blank and I believed her. Wanted to believe her. Told myself I believed her." He got down to the real truth at last and hated himself for it. "I pretended to myself that I believed her. See? Shoot! This is where I ask myself what the hell? What was I doing? What was I thinking? Just what…the…*hell?*"

"Don't." She had that caring, stricken look on her face

again, and Maddie and Holly were splashing and happy, oblivious in the pool.

"You don't know." Again, her level of care almost made him angry, because he didn't deserve it. "I *wanted* to believe her, against the evidence, because I wanted my life back! That's the truth. I loved the girls. Of course I did. But it was hard, and she was their mother, and the mother gets the babies when two people split up that soon after the birth."

"How old were they?"

"Three months. Still pretty small. And I let her have them. I'll never forgive myself for that."

"What about her parents?"

"They were on my side. Still are. They gave her so much love. The generous kind. The tough kind. The practical kind. None of it helped. In the end, they had to step back. They're in Louisiana now, where their other two kids are, and their other grandchildren—all doing well, which is great—so it's hard to see them often, but we're in touch a lot."

"So you said the girls were with their mother when they were three months old?"

"Yes, but by the time they were five months old she was living with her dealer—*Don't!*" he interrupted himself, way too quick and harsh, but he couldn't let her keep doing the sounds of sympathy and understanding, and the heartfelt looking at him with her big, lovely, blue-green eyes. They kept saying this to each other.

*Don't.*

Warning each other away from the wrong response.

"Don't say anything nice, Mary Jane. Please. Don't let me off the hook."

"Okay. Sorry." Her cheeks had gone pink.

"And don't apologize. And *ignore* me biting your head off. *Please*. If you can."

"Trying."

"Thanks. Anyhow… Don't know how old they were when she moved in with her pimp. Nine months? By then I knew I had to get them back, get them away, give them a future and a father who was worth something. But it wasn't that easy. I started a law degree. That was what kept me in California for so long, even once I had sole custody. I waited to graduate, which I did this past May."

"Oh, wow. Congratulations!"

"Thanks." He couldn't see it as a big deal. He'd done it for the girls, because he'd failed them when they were babies. "Took me six years to get through the degree, part-time. Came back here as soon as I could after that, to be closer to Dad and my brothers, and just to protect the girls. Taking the New York bar exam soon. Don't know if I'll pass," he admitted truthfully. He wasn't getting as much time to study for it as he needed.

"You will," she said. Of course she said that. He could see the belief shining in her eyes, and it almost made him cry. She had no reason to show such faith. He wasn't worth it, was he? Thinking back on how he'd let the girls down after their birth always made him doubt himself until he was raw with it.

"So the law degree helped me understand the court battle. Which was horrible. And long. And expensive. I'm not going to give you the blow-by-blow. I can't. It's all a tangle, can't even remember, there were so many ugly steps in the whole saga."

"They never see her?"

"Nope. There was a supervised-access arrangement for a while, but she violated that so many times, she lost it in the end, and I wasn't sorry. In fact I pushed for it. If you could see her… She looks like what she is. What she's become. You wouldn't believe she could ever have been a model. It's— Yeah. I'm not letting the girls anywhere near that. I still have nightmares about their safety. You know that horrible kind where you're running and running but can't move, or that you're trapped somewhere. I've dreamed I lost them in airports, or that they're running across a railroad track and there's a train bearing down on them and I'm trying to warn them and my voice won't work."

"Oh, Joe!" She was doing it again. She wasn't anywhere near as beautiful as the girls' mother had once been—not many women were—but right at this moment she looked to Joe like the loveliest woman in the world because of the emotion in her eyes and the hope in her heart and the clear health in her body and skin and hair, when he still had images of the girls' mother's raddled and bone-skinny and prematurely aged appearance in his mind.

Wait a minute, though. Hope in her heart? Hope for what?

Yes, okay, he could see it. He knew. He'd thought about this just last night at dinner. He'd been a player long enough. She liked him. She was pulling toward him like a magnet, and quite possibly she didn't even know it.

*Don't do this, Mary Jane,* he wanted to tell her.

She was too nice and too generous. He liked her too much to give her the automatic come-on that once would have been second nature to him, to say yes to the unconscious invitation in her eyes. Those days seemed like a life-time ago.

Well, they *were* a lifetime ago. Maddie and Holly's lifetime.

In the seven years since their birth and his split from their mother, he'd had—didn't take long to work it out— exactly one girlfriend.

Five years ago.

She'd lasted for three months of his working around the clock, his battles to find the right child care, his late nights falling asleep over law books, his dropping everything for the next painful round of family court appearances, before she'd had enough of his life and they'd called it quits.

He was a player? Really?

It suddenly occurred to him that he'd totally forgotten how, it was so long ago and he was such a different person now. Anything and everything he thought he saw in Mary Jane's eyes might be a complete figment of his desperate and celibate imagination, a sad throwback to his long-gone high school popularity.

Catching himself just in time, he didn't lift the hand that had been poised to reach out and touch her. He didn't give her the slow, deliberate smile that had once worked so well. He wanted to jeer at himself for even thinking about it.

All that feeling in Mary Jane's eyes was because of the girls, not him, and that was just the way it should be.

For the new, improved Joe Capelli—the Joe he was now, not the Joe he'd been seven, ten, sixteen years ago—everything, *always,* was all about the girls.

## Chapter Seven

Holly and Maddie were getting cold, Mary Jane could see.

The sun had started to dip behind the trees, leaving the pool in dappled shade, and even though the water was warmed several degrees by the solar pool heater they'd installed on the restaurant roof a few months ago, it wasn't enough to compensate for the chill of the breeze on the girls' wet skin every time they clambered out of the water in order to jump back in.

Their new friends were about to leave, also, giving a last wave as they went through the gate, wrapped in their colorful towels.

"Time to get them home," Joe said.

"Yes, before their lips turn from purple to blue."

"Is that the direction it goes?" he joked. "Is blue colder than purple?" It was a little forced.

He'd shared a huge amount, been incredibly honest, made himself very, very vulnerable, and he was probably regretting it. People often did.

Mary Jane was.

Or, no, regretting was too strong. More like second-guessing, wondering about the things she'd said in reply, the reactions she'd shown. Did he realize what a powerful story it was, and what a vivid picture he'd painted? Did he know how much she'd been able to read between the lines? How much it said about his tenacity and determination and care? About his self-condemnation? And did he know he'd never once spoken Holly and Maddie's mother's name?

That, she suspected he did. It seemed like a deliberate avoidance, as if the sound of the syllables was too painful, and Mary Jane understood this. She'd spent quite some time not being able to say the word *Alex,* and had come up with all sorts of alternatives in her head, to keep her mind off the subject.

She could say it now.

Alex, Alex, Alex. There! No power to hurt, or to catapult her back into the past.

She thought that, for Joe, everything must still be a lot more fresh and raw, a lot more painful, since he'd had so much more to deal with.

"Blue is definitely colder," she said, deliberately trying to keep it light.

"Time to get out, girls," he called to them, and they did so at once, causing him to observe, "I think you're right. Blue is colder, because their lips have transitioned fully to blue now, and they're not arguing."

"Would they like some hot chocolate to warm them up before you head home? I can easily fix them some, up in the kitchen."

She thought he'd say no, but when he looked at them shivering in their towels, he nodded. "It would help, if it's really not too much trouble. They'll have to get dressed.

Back in the office, where they put on their swimsuits before?"

"No, just come upstairs. It's a four-bedroom apartment. They can use a bedroom or bathroom."

"Better be the bathroom. They're still pretty wet."

The girls darted across in their bare feet, still wrapped tightly in their towels and still shivering. They left wet footprints on the hardwood stairs, just the way Mary Jane and Lee and Daisy used to do when they were kids, and then, after instructions from Joe, they disappeared into the bathroom to get dressed, along with the backpacks where they'd placed their clothes, while Joe followed Mary Jane into the kitchen.

Into the kitchen that she'd grown up with and that had always seemed quite spacious, but was now suddenly far too small.

She turned her back to him. Well, it was the natural thing to do, rummaging in the pantry for the container of drinking chocolate powder which she began to fear was just a figment of her imagination. Had they run out? She found it at last, all the way in the back, and even turned up an unopened packet of mini pink and white marshmallows, then had to turn away from Joe again to get the milk out of the fridge.

She poured it into two mugs, incredibly self-conscious about the way he was watching her, leaning one shoulder against the corner of the fridge, not speaking very much, and making her heart beat faster just by being there.

"Thanks for this," he said gruffly. "For all of it. The camp arrangement. Listening to me. Taking care of the girls."

"No problem, honestly."

Or if it was a problem, not in the way he thought. Something seemed to have switched on inside her, a warmth she'd lost in recent years. She'd hated that—hated the steely thread of bitterness that seemed to have replaced it.

Silence again, while his eyes followed her movements as she came to put the milk away. He had to shift position, which he did in a heavy way that told her he was tired. Wrung-out, probably, after all that he'd said out by the pool.

Why couldn't she think of something to talk about? They'd covered so much ground today. She already felt as if she knew him so much better.

Maybe that was why. The things he'd shared weren't exactly the basis for casual conversation. The silence between them was thick with their shared awareness of how much she knew. Silence was much harder than words.

*Think of something, Mary Jane! Don't make this worse by having him think he's done the wrong thing in talking. Find a way.*

Picking up the milk-filled mugs to put them in the microwave to heat, she looked up at him, and that was a mistake. A big one. All the helplessness showed in her eyes, she knew it, and there was something in his eyes, too. Maybe exactly the same thing.

Helplessness.

Need.

Connection.

It just happened. One moment everything was fine, she was about to put the mugs of milk into the microwave, and the next moment the mugs were back on the countertop and she and Joe had simply come together, folded into each other, softened and melted and fused, the fabric of their clothing the only thing keeping them from losing all boundaries between their two bodies.

It went from zero to sixty so fast. One light, questing touch from his lips, and then full-on—arms wrapped around each other, her hair streaked against his face, her mouth as eager and giving as his, her breath rapidly quickening.

He kissed the way she knew he would. Like a dream. Slow and soft and intent, as if her mouth was the only thing he knew in the world. Hungry, as if he hadn't kissed a woman in years. Expert, as if once upon a time he'd trained for this and aced the test.

She knew all about that—the girls in high school and since, the practiced lines—and right now she didn't care. Didn't think she could ever care. That was all in the past, and if he was still that guy, then she was still the foolish woman who'd waited years for Alex to finally answer her blunt challenge and turn her down.

And she knew she wasn't that woman anymore.

Right now, she was a woman who wanted this and nothing more. Just a steaming, sizzling, fabulous kiss with a gorgeous man, and she would think about all the rest later.

Or not.

Maybe she'd never think about it. Maybe she wouldn't have to. Who cared?

Kissing Joe Capelli, nothing else seemed to matter. It was a moment out of time, frozen, endless, wondrous. It wasn't about her high school mix of crush and loathing, although that had been powerful enough. It wasn't about what he'd told her about the girls and his battle for their safety, although her heart still ached for him over all of that.

The only thing that mattered was that she wanted it, and he did, too, and it felt good.

She tightened her arms around him and felt the hot, hard weight of his groin against her body. He tried to ease it away, embarrassed maybe, but she wouldn't let him, and cupped her hands against his butt to keep him in place. He groaned. She muffled the groan with her mouth and felt the vibration of it in his chest, that dark baritone voice of his like the rumble of a warm engine on a dark summer night.

He touched her, sliding his hands down to her hips and holding them lightly, then moving them up until he reached the weight of the undersides of her breasts, where he seemed to want to stop, nudging a little, caressing, feeling the heaviness and liking it, she thought.

And then, when she wasn't remotely prepared for it and didn't know what had triggered it or what had changed, he stopped kissing her and tore his beautiful mouth away, to whisper, "I'm so sorry." He tried to let her go.

"Don't be. Why?"

"I didn't want to do this. I told myself I wouldn't."

"Told yourself. So you were thinking about it?"

"Yes." The admission seemed to drag itself out of him with incredible weight.

"That's okay. So was I. I want it." She couldn't find fancy words, just the truth.

"You're too nice." Again, he tried to pull away.

She wasn't having that. "What if I don't want to be nice?" She levered him against her body again, using her hands to pull that tight butt toward her and squash herself into his hardness.

He said, shaky and distracted—Good, she wanted him distracted!—"You don't have much choice about being nice. You just are."

She traced a fingertip over the fine line where his full top lip met his slightly beard-roughened face, wondering where this was coming from in her. He chased the fingertip with his mouth and she dropped her hand to cup his jaw instead. Mmm, it felt good. She'd gone crazy, and it seemed as if she'd been waiting her whole life to do that.

He'd started it, but she'd more than caught up, and she wasn't going to let him tell her this wasn't good for her.

It was.

"Is that why you're doing this?" she murmured, inches from his mouth, letting her breath whisper against his skin. "Because I'm nice."

"No," he said bluntly. "I'm doing it because you're hot. Right now, you seem like the hottest woman I've ever seen. Not sure where you put all the heat, because normally it doesn't show, but right now…"

"Right now, stop talking. Please?"

He muttered something under his breath and mashed his mouth gloriously against hers once more. She laughed, and he wanted to know why, whispering the question into her mouth.

She couldn't tell him.

Didn't really know.

Just because this felt good, and delicious, and because for once she wasn't thinking of complications and problems, second-guessing her own reactions or his. It just felt so, so good, and wasn't that rare, and a miracle, and something to laugh about in a state of beautiful glee?

"I'm laughing because I'm happy about this," she finally decided out loud.

"About me kissing you."

"Yes. Simple, really."

"Simple is nice. Strange…"

"Because we haven't had it in so long, either of us. That's why it's strange."

"You're right." This time, he was the one laughing. "You're so right!"

In that joyous spirit, he kissed her some more.

Until he thought of something, minutes later. "Those girls have been gone too long. They should have been dressed ages ago." This time, there was nothing half-hearted in the way he pulled back. "I need to find out what they're up to. Shoot!" He looked Mary Jane up and down, a smoking hot, intimate look that said he was surprised and pleased and seeing her in a whole new light.

She blushed at that thought. She was seeing herself in a whole new light, too.

But then he disappeared from the kitchen and reality began to kick in. She followed him in the direction of the bathroom, and he was a few strides away from turning in through the open doorway when they both heard a crash and the frightened exclamations and frantic recriminations of two seven-year-old girls.

"You let it go!"

"You were holding it!"

"No, I wasn't! I was giving it to you!"

There was quite a scene awaiting Joe and Mary Jane. Once dressed, Holly and Maddie had apparently decided to explore the bathroom cabinets and play with Mary Jane's makeup and skin-care creams, which were sitting in piles and rows all over the floor. She was quite fond of her skin-care creams. That crash had been the very most expensive one she had, housed in a gorgeous frosted glass container with an ornate embossed lid, falling onto the tiles with predictable results.

The girls stood frozen and horrified in the middle of the mess, their faces daubed with little experiments in color and texture and scent.

Joe was—

Joe was more horrified than he needed to be. Almost at once, Mary Jane stopped minding about the mess and breakage and started minding about his reaction far more.

"Girls... Ah hell, girls... Shoot! *Jeesh.* What have you been doing? Could you not hold it together just a few minutes longer?" He pressed the heels of his hands against the sides of his head, and his voice was anguished. "Mary Jane, I can't even start with the apologies."

"I crashed your car yesterday," she reminded him, for the second time that day.

"Yeah, but… No. Hell. We talked before, remember? This scares me. Girls, we're going to clean this up right now. And your faces. We're going to stay here until it's perfect. And you're going to pay for the broken jar and any mess in the makeup by doing chores, and your wages are going to be pretty low, I'm telling you! What were you *doing?*"

"We didn't mean to drop it."

"Yeah, but you shouldn't have been touching it in the first place. You shouldn't have been touching any of this. Opening the jars. Putting lipstick on. You shouldn't even have opened the cabinet. What have we said? Lots of times? About touching other people's stuff? You were so good today at Penelope's. Do we have to cancel pony camp? Are you going to do this kind of thing there?"

"No!"

"No, Daddy!"

Their voices came in a tangle of shared sentences and alternating pleas.

"Don't cancel pony camp!"

"Please don't cancel pony camp!"

"We just wanted to look."

"We were *appreciating* it."

"We weren't trying to mess with it."

"And then we thought Mary Jane wouldn't mind if we had a little try."

"Of the lipstick and the cream."

"She has such pretty bottles and jars and stuff."

"Because we don't have a mom to let us play with hers."

"Amber said she plays with her mom's, and it sounds so fun."

"And then we…"

"…kind of forgot…"

"…that they weren't ours."

"And that Mary Jane hadn't said that we could touch."

He turned to Mary Jane, his face a mask of anguish that seemed too much. "Can you go, while we clean up? Can you trust me to supervise this?"

"Of course."

"Go relax, or whatever you need to do. I'm not taking your time over this. I shouldn't have—" He cut himself off, and she knew what he was thinking about.

He shouldn't have kissed her.

She didn't agree. She most definitely thought that he should have kissed her. Kissed her longer. Made a plan for kissing her again.

"I should have kept better track of how long they'd been gone," he finished.

"If you're going to play that game," she told him, "so should I."

"You don't know them like I do."

"They're just ki—"

"No. Don't let them off the hook. Go. The mugs are still sitting there on the bench. Pour the milk back into the container. They're not getting those hot chocolates now!"

"Really, they can—"

"No. There have to be consequences."

He was their dad, and he was going to stay firm, Mary Jane could see. She went away, reluctantly—but what else could she do? She had an insight into his fears, now, after everything he'd told her today about their mother's poor impulse control and compulsively self-destructive behavior. Those words about not having a mom must have torn his heart in pieces.

There was a long way to travel between dropping a jar of "borrowed" skin cream at the age of seven and stealing money for drugs at the age of thirty-one, but she could understand why Joe feared his girls making that journey, and why he was tough on them sometimes because of it. Was he right to think that firm parenting now would help keep them on the right course?

Beyond the brief episode of naughtiness, they were such gorgeous girls, she'd lost her heart to them already…and to their father. She didn't want to see them punished, but she knew that was probably too soft, too sentimental. It seemed so much easier to let them off the hook, and Joe wasn't about the easy road in the parenting department, he'd been doing it tough for a while, and he wasn't dropping that ball.

She understood.

And she wanted to make it better for all three of them anyhow.

Twenty minutes passed before Joe and the girls appeared again. Mary Jane had put the milk and chocolate powder and marshmallows away, and was pretending to sit on the couch reading a book, because he'd told her to "relax" so she felt that she should.

"All done," he announced. "The girls have something to say."

*They don't have to.*

But she didn't say it, just nodded as she stood up and faced them formally, because once again she understood what Joe was trying to do.

They were formal about it, also. "We're very sorry we messed with your stuff," they said together. "We won't ever do it again, and we'll pay for the cream."

"Thank you for such a nice apology," she told them.

"Go wait for me in the car, okay?" Joe said, and they picked up their damp-looking backpacks and went out of the living room and down the stairs. After they were out of earshot, he asked, "How much for the skin cream?"

She didn't dare tell him. It was a top-of-the-range product, an indulgence on her part, and was priced to match. "Just make it twenty dollars."

"Come on!"

"The jar wasn't full."

"Even I, as a mere male, know it would have cost more than that, if it had been three-quarters empty. Which it wasn't. And there was the lipstick and other stuff they used."

"Joe, I don't want them slaving away to replace it. I know it's right that they should compensate in some way for the breakage, but they shouldn't have to pay for my frivolity in treating myself to that brand."

"Twenty dollars *each*. And I'll pay them a dollar each every time they wash dishes or vacuum."

She nodded, because if they kept arguing about it, she'd end up telling him what it really cost and he'd probably collapse on the floor.

He did one of those mutters under his breath that said he was close to the end of his rope, and she realized his life must have been like this for years, a continuous procession from minor incident to major disaster and back again, none of it his fault, despite what he thought, despite that damning description he'd given her, filled with self-disgust—"two beautiful people trying to get famous."

He shifted his weight, as if trying to make up his mind about something, or find the words for something, without having much success. He seemed to do the weight-shifting thing a lot, as if he was restless every time he wasn't doing productive work, and the impatient movement seemed like a testament to his crammed and disciplined schedule.

"Do you need to go?" she asked him, wanting to smooth the way for him. Again. It was starting to become a habit. "The girls are in the car…"

"Probably should. And they'd just better be in the car!"

"They will be."

"They will, yes. This time. Because they've just been yelled at. They wouldn't dare go off exploring. Still, yes, I need to get going."

But he didn't move. And they were both thinking about that kiss, she knew. The memory of it hung thick in the air between them, making her pulses beat faster and her breathing grow shallower. When she looked at him, all she could focus on was his mouth, but that was bad… foolish…so she kept dragging her gaze away and didn't know where to look instead.

He didn't say anything, but he didn't move to leave, either, and the seconds stretched. "Uh, Mary Jane… Yeah." He lifted his hand to the back of his head, a gesture that told her he was still lost for words.

So apparently it was up to her to raise the subject. "What was that all about just now, Joe?" she said very carefully. "I'm sorry. I have to ask. I mean, I assume that's why you're still here. We…didn't really finish."

He gave her a fleeting look, too powerful considering the fraction of a second it lasted. It felt as if he could see right into her, and as if he *wanted* to. "I don't know what it was about. The wrong things, probably."

"Why?"

"Just happened, didn't it?"

"I mean, why were they the wrong things?"

"Two people wondering where their lives went, grabbing onto something because it felt good."

*What?*

Her rebellion was instant. "No! I'm not taking that lying down, Joe! I don't believe it for a second! Is that us? Is that all we are? All it was?" He'd shocked her with the bluntness of the words, and she knew he'd done it on purpose.

To distance them both from something that left him uncomfortable, something he didn't want. Or didn't *want* to want? Which?

"No, it's not all. Of course it's not." The words were filled with meaning. "There is a heck of a lot more."

"Good!"

He gave her one last suffering look. "But I don't think I can let it be any of those other things."

## Chapter Eight

He left.

She wanted so much to hold him in place with the right words or the right action, but nothing came, and in the end she just watched him turn around and walk out of the room with that suffering look still on his face.

She listened to his footsteps all the way down the stairs, heard the office door close behind him, then the car door, then the car engine, and finally its fade into silence.

It hadn't been much more than twenty-four hours since she'd taken her car into Capelli Auto and seen that pair of male legs sticking out from under a vehicle, yet she felt as if her heart had covered about a thousand miles.

A thousand miles of emotional journey.

A thousand miles of life.

She hadn't really loathed him in high school. She'd had a massive crush that she hadn't admitted even to herself. Like every other girl, she'd thought he was gorgeous and cool, and her teenage hormones had been held hostage to his raw male appeal despite everything her good sense had insisted on.

But she wasn't in high school anymore. She was a grown woman.

No, worse, she was a woman staring down the onset of middle age, without any of the satisfactions in her life that she'd once thought middle age would bring. What had Joe said just now?

*Two people wondering where their lives went.*

She'd fought him on that, and on what it meant, but really he was right. Where had her life gone? Not down the road she'd thought it would, and now she was here, and Joe had slid out from under an engine and into the picture with those motherless girls of his and Mary Jane had fallen so far and hard and fast for all three of them that she could barely breathe.

Twenty-four hours. Twenty-seven, max.

Did she have the same good sense she'd had in high school? Surely she ought to have more!

She could not *possibly* think about putting herself into the cute picture that was Joe with his girls. She didn't belong there, and it was just a fantasy. Gorgeous man, readymade family, people who needed her.

*There, Mary Jane, isn't that the heart of the problem? They need a nurturing woman in their lives and you're a total soft touch for that.*

And it probably showed.

Joe could probably see it all too clearly, and if he wanted to use it—use her—then he easily could.

*No, Mary Jane, don't tell yourself that he's not that kind of man. How would you know?*

Alex had used her for years and she hadn't seen it until the bitter end. Until *after* the bitter end. Did she trust herself to pick up on the same thing in Joe, when her yearning for a family blinded her as much now as it had blinded her with Alex?

She had no idea.

The parts for Mary Jane's car arrived the next day.

At eight in the morning Joe delivered the girls to the Richardsons' housekeeping cottage at Spruce Bay and spent a half hour getting to know Vanessa and Phil, nanny Lucy and the two children, eight-year-old Jessica and six-year-old Simon.

Phil was English, like Penelope, but Vanessa was American, and they'd met through their shared involvement in equestrian competition. Clearly, they'd both grown up with much privilege and family money, but they somehow managed to be reasonably down-to-earth in spite of it.

Meanwhile, Dad was manning the garage, dealing with the clients who were dropping their vehicles in today for service and repair, which meant that Joe had enough time to reassure himself that the new arrangement was off to a good start.

Vanessa and Phil were both wiry and very fit in their expensive-looking English-style jodhpurs, but the two children just wore jeans, so Holly and Maddie weren't out of place. Lucy seemed friendly and sensible, and he contented himself with one half joke of a warning. "Watch these two! They're not as innocent as they look!"

Lucy just laughed.

The Richardsons had come from Kentucky with two vehicles. They had their massive ten-horse trailer currently parked at Penelope's, and a seven-seater SUV which they used for driving around locally. Maddie and Holly put their daypacks in the back of it and Lucy and the Richardsons climbed in with them and drove away, leaving Joe to remind himself firmly that the girls had been to babysitters and child-care centers their whole lives and nothing seriously terrible had happened yet.

Still, he stood there for longer than he needed to, watching the SUV disappear behind the trees that lined Spruce Bay Resort's long driveway, before he stirred himself to leave. There'd been no sign of Mary Jane this morning. He could go look for her, of course—nothing stopping him. But it didn't seem like a good idea, so he left it, and tried not to stare over in the direction of the office and attached family apartment. If she was anywhere near a window and saw him looking…

But when he arrived back at the garage, there were her car parts. He would hopefully have time to begin tackling the vehicle today, which would mean he'd finish it tomorrow, and he might get as far as starting on the car she'd crashed, by the weekend.

He worked hard all day, and thought he'd probably be able to call Mary Jane midmorning tomorrow to tell her she could collect her car.

At four o'clock, he went to pick up the girls.

"How was it, pumpkins?" he asked them once he'd said thanks to Lucy and hi to Jessica and Simon, and had the girls safely in the car. Vanessa and Phil were still at Penelope's, working with their horses.

"It was fabulous, fabulous, fabulous," Holly said.

"And wonderful, wonderful, wonderful," Maddie agreed.

"Only that good?" he returned mildly. "I thought you might like it a little more than that."

They thought this was hilarious.

"So tell me," he invited them, and received a blow-by-blow description of their day that lasted all the way home.

They were wiped that night. He ordered them into the

bath before dinner, while he finished grilling some Italian sausages and setting out store-bought potato salad and coleslaw. After the meal, they just had enough energy left for him to sit with them and read out loud. Really, their reading was good enough that he didn't need to do this anymore, but it anchored the end of their day with something quiet and close for all three of them. They weren't ready to give it up yet, and neither was he.

Tonight, he refused to read them anything about ponies. "Now that you're riding real ponies, you don't need to read about other girls doing it." So they started on *The Lion, the Witch and the Wardrobe* instead.

They could barely keep their eyes open until the end of the first chapter, and when he'd left their bedroom it was still early enough that he went to his law books and practice tests with more energy and enthusiasm than he'd managed in weeks. Since Dad had had a quiet, restorative day he insisted on clearing up the meal, and Joe didn't argue because every minute of studying for that bar exam gave him a better chance of passing it.

Friday worked out just as well.

Joe delivered the girls, fixed cars and called Mary Jane when hers was ready. Once again, he hadn't seen her at Spruce Bay this morning and he wondered about that.

If she was avoiding him.

If he minded.

If he would kiss her again the moment he had the slightest chance.

No answers sprang to mind on any of the above.

She was warmly grateful about the repair job. "Oh, it's done? Already? You thought it might take longer."

"The parts arrived promptly, which was a big help. You can pick it up whenever you like. I'll be here until five."

"Let me have a think about how I'm going to organize it,

with returning the rental car." Her voice was a little more distant and formal now, down the line, as if she wasn't happy with the way she'd sounded before. "Do I need to give you an exact time?"

"No, just get here when you get here." He resisted the temptation to help her out by driving her vehicle to the car rental place and meeting her there, because the kissing thing was filling his mind too much, and he didn't trust it. He didn't want to do anything that might strengthen their personal connection, if her coolness was a signal that she wanted to get back on a business footing again.

"Really?" she said. "That's great, because we're pretty busy here today."

"Vanessa and Phil are dropping the girls home this afternoon," he said, "because they're all going mini golfing later this afternoon, so I'll be here without a break all afternoon."

"Great!" she repeated. "Thanks." And that was the end of the call.

She came at four.

From the office, he saw a teenage girl in an old Ford Escort drop her out front and then zoom away with a quick wave. The distance Mary Jane then had to travel to reach the office gave him plenty of time to wonder about how they were going to handle each other and not nearly enough time to make any decisions about it.

When she came through the doorway, he saw exactly the same uncertainty reflected in her own expression.

And he really hadn't intended to answer her unspoken questions in the way he did, but it happened anyway. She came toward him with her purse open, hanging from its strap on her shoulder, and her attention suddenly focused on taking out her credit card as if she didn't want to meet his eye, and he just slid the purse strap off her shoulder, dropped it on the floor and moved in on her mouth with unwavering intent.

*Jiminy!*

They hadn't said a word to each other. It was all in their bodies, their lips, their hands. She gave one cry of surprise but didn't fight him for a second. She wanted it as much as he did. Her enthusiasm was blind and hungry and wonderful. No coaxing or cajoling required. She melted into him, and she was so soft and luscious, he was throbbing within seconds.

It was a deep, hot kiss. He ran the tip of his tongue along the seam of her lips to coax them open, but she was way ahead of him, parting them and panting out a breath against his skin. He ran his fingers into her hair, and let them tangle them there, loving the silk of it and the sweet, floral scent released into the air.

He let his eyes close in blissful need, then opened them again so he could look at her. So close. A blur. Dark crescents of lash against her pink cheeks. Pale ear sticking out like a pixie's from the streams of hair. Neck he wanted to kiss, too, except he couldn't take himself away from her mouth.

She rocked her hips and he moved with her and they bumped the countertop and knocked a pen to the floor. He moved again and trod on it. It gave a plasticky crunch under his work boot, which they both ignored because the kiss was too intense and too demanding.

They were standing in a garage, for heck's sake!

Okay, the garage office, but it was pretty much the same thing. Nowhere soft to sit. Nowhere to get comfortable and private. Not even a clutter-free surface where he could sit her so she could wrap her legs around him and—

Hell! Was he seriously contemplating having sex with this woman right here and now?

Well, yes, now that you mention it…

*Joe Capelli, get yourself under control!*

Nope, not yet.

He kissed her some more. Took it a little further than kissing and she went with him on this, too. When he ran his probably-too-rough-for-her fingers up under the soft stretch cotton of her top in search of her breasts, she arched her back and let him find them. She gave them to him, gasping when his cupped hands closed over their fullness.

Shoot, he wished she wasn't wearing a bra!

Still, the bra was nice. Very, very nice. All lacy and shapely and low-cut in front. He could run his thumbs along the edge of the fabric, where her skin was so tender and soft, and feel the push of her hardened nipples against his palms, through the lace.

He wondered what color it was. He wondered if all her bras felt this nice, or if they felt even better. If she had satin ones, smooth ones, bras cut even lower, bras that pushed her breasts higher. He wondered what she would do if he reached around and unfastened this one, and in a moment of pure maleness, he took the question to the experimental phase before it was even fully formed in his mind.

The hook was tricky. She didn't help, but she didn't stop him, either. He finally managed it and received his reward. Those breasts. In his hands. Touch making her shudder. Her skin there was so delicate and tender and warm and soft. The weight of her moved with him. Nothing fake about these.

Nothing fake about any of her, and he wanted to discover it all, with nothing getting in the way. The silky curve of her butt, the knobs of her spine and shoulders, the slightly squishy part of her lower stomach that she probably thought should be harder and flatter. He didn't agree.

Maybe if he just swept all this paper off the counter-top...

Not possible.

He had one more client coming in to pick up a car—a guy he and Mary Jane both knew from high school. He really could not sweep Steve Wright's invoice onto the floor so he could pull up Mary Jane's floaty skirt and twist her panties out of the way and make love to her on the laminate.

In pain, he let her go, pulling his mouth out of their kiss like a pilot pulling a plane out of a dive, releasing her breasts so that they fell a little and bounced—ah, hell, yes, they really did, and it was spectacular—against the fabric of her top. Her nipples were like hard little buttons pro-claiming her state of arousal and he loved that.

So tough to pull back!

"This isn't the place," he said. "Wish it was, but it's not."

"No." She hunched her shoulders, opposite to the arch-ing movement she'd made earlier. She was hiding herself now, instead of giving herself to him. With some trem-bling clumsiness and embarrassment, she refastened the bra, while he watched. "What were we thinking?"

"Not very much." But he didn't want to backpedal all that far. He didn't regret this. "Come out with me tonight. Let's do this properly."

"I'm not sure..." she began, but he wouldn't let her hesi-tate and doubt and second-guess them both out of this now. His own doubts had been swept away by the strength of their connection.

This meant something.

He wanted it.

Needed it.

"I'm sure," he told her. "We have something here. I don't

know what it is, but it's something and if we don't follow through on it, this'll keep happening."

"Will it?"

"Hell, yes! I'll come looking for you at Spruce Bay when I drop off the girls. There are all those beds in all those motel rooms and cottages and cabins. And don't try to tell me you won't be waiting for it. So let's agree that we're doing it and do it properly, rather than pretend we're not doing it, and do it anyhow, and end up in a mess."

She nodded. "Okay."

"Okay?"

"Okay, I won't try to tell you that I'm not waiting for it. Okay, we'll have dinner. Okay, we'll do it properly so we don't end up in a mess."

*Yes!*

Fist pump!

*Wait, Joe.*

He remembered Dad and the girls, and that he wasn't in high school anymore, and hadn't been for a long time. His head and heart knew that perfectly well, but his body was slow to learn in a situation like this.

A situation he hadn't even been tempted to put himself in for a long time.

"Can I call you?" he said.

"Call me?"

"I have to make sure it's going to work with Dad. I'll be asking him to watch the girls. Which should be fine as long as they're asleep. Can we make it a late meal? Eight?"

"That suits me, too. I need to make sure things are running smoothly for Daisy and her crew, and that I have someone for the office."

"I'll check with Dad and you'll hear from me as soon as I know. The minute I know."

She smiled—laughed, really—and tilted her head to

look at him as if he was being cute. He couldn't work out why until he took a pause for breath and realized he was acting like the world was about to end and he had to seal the deal in the next three seconds or never. "Call when you can. It's fine," she said.

"Yeah, I guess it is," he muttered, embarrassed—a little— but smiling just like she was, because…

Well, just because.

Because they'd kissed.

More than kissed.

And it had felt good, and even though they'd stopped, it still felt good, and she didn't seem to be in any doubt about coming out with him tonight, and so far she seemed to like the girls, which was important, incredibly important, and it was so long since he'd had this…felt this…

Had he ever felt this?

It was just kind of warm and tickly and made his breathing feel like an overinflated balloon. He was giddy with it, dizzy with relief and exultation. The past few years had been so hard.

He needed a break.

He needed a woman.

He needed Mary Jane.

The other client arrived. Steve, from school. Mary Jane caught sight of him and the expression on her face said that she knew him at once. Well, they'd both stayed in the area. She'd probably run into him a few times since school, or maybe even kept up contact. She wouldn't have had the same struggle to recognize the guy that Joe had had.

Steve was a big man, once a star on the football team. He'd talked of playing at college level and maybe even professionally, but he'd blown his football scholarship in his first year at Ohio State with a failing GPA. But he hadn't stopped eating when he'd stopped exercising. It really showed now. The drinking showed even more.

Mary Jane didn't want to run into him today, it was clear. Seconds before Steve arrived in the office, she'd darted through the connecting door into the service area, where Joe had a car up on the lift and it made a handy shield for her to hide behind.

"Thanks, buddy," Steve said after Joe had put the payment through.

"No problem. It was a little overdue this time. The oil looked pretty dirty. It'll run better and save you money on gas if you bring it in on schedule. I put a sticker on the windshield, with the mileage and date."

"Yeah, that stuff gets away from us sometimes, and money's pretty tight. Kids cost more and more the older they get!"

"Isn't that the truth?" Joe agreed.

Steve seemed as if he was about to leave, but then he paused. "Hey...nice that you're back in the area. Hollywood plan didn't work out, huh?" He was trying to sound neutral about it, or even sympathetic, but Joe caught the clear lick of satisfaction behind the words.

So the big dreams hadn't panned out? *Welcome to my world,* Steve was clearly thinking. *It's where you belong, and I'm glad you know it now.*

"No, they didn't," Joe agreed. He could have added more. That he had no regrets. Or that he had a law degree and was about to take the New York bar exam. He wasn't exactly living in the gutter, despite his various regrets. But he stayed silent.

It wasn't a competition. He had nothing to prove. He'd once cared a whole lot about what his peers thought of him, but he didn't anymore, and he counted that a victory.

"That's too bad," Steve said.

"Yeah, it is."

"I'm real sorry to hear it." He was practically grinning about it now.

*Please don't suggest that we have a drink together sometime.*

Maybe Joe was putting more frost into the air than he thought, because the unwanted invitation didn't come.

"See you when that odometer kicks around again," Steve said. "It'll probably be sooner than I want."

"Good to catch up."

"Yeah, it was." Steve left at last.

Mary Jane emerged from her hiding place, brushing her palms down her skirt and tidying her hair as if she felt dirty and a mess. She didn't look it. She looked adorable… terrific. Cheeks still a little pink. Hair still tumbled. Self-consciousness giving her a human warmth that Joe responded to with a hunger he hadn't known was in him.

"Sorry 'bout that," he said to her.

"Sorry I hid. Steve is a pest, and always has been. I run into him occasionally."

"Thought you might."

"He's always really happy to hear about other people's shattered dreams. Makes him feel better about his own."

"Yeah, I got that, too."

She laughed. "Oh, wow! So obvious?"

"Maybe I'm just incredibly perceptive."

"Maybe you are…" She gave him a sly grin, this time.

"So…tonight," he told her, needing it more, now. Wanting it more.

"Yes. Tonight." There was a power in the two simple words that suggested she felt the same.

## Chapter Nine

It was the age-old female problem, Mary Jane decided, looking in her closet.

What to wear?

Joe had confirmed the dinner plan on the phone after talking to his father, but he hadn't said anything about where they might go, or whether he'd made a reservation. She had no idea if he was picturing a fancy restaurant meal or wings and nachos in a bar, and the whole thing was complicated by her doubts about the signals she wanted to send.

Was it really about signals? Hadn't she already signaled quite a bit?

Too much.

She felt her own vulnerability like an ache in her bones. Like nakedness. If Joe had picked up so fast on Steve Wright's malicious pleasure in other people's life failings, then he would have no trouble picking up on how much she yearned for what he had, and what he had to offer.

What was that phrase, "low-hanging fruit"?

That was her. Ripe and red and ready to fall into his hand without him even having to reach for her. It wasn't a sin or a crime or a fault, not at heart. She did know that. It came from the best things about her. She had a lot of love to give, and not enough people to give it to, and she felt thwarted by this, deprived of the best chance to be who she was.

It made her…well, all the things she'd felt before.

Naked.

Vulnerable.

Wanting.

And there seemed to be nothing she could do about it, because she'd been trying from the very start Tuesday evening.

Lee was downstairs right now, staffing the office for the evening. Mary Jane had told her what was happening, who she was going out with tonight, and Lee had whistled.

Which was so unfair!

Lee should know what this was like after her big dramatic romance with Mac so recently—having a baby on the way before they even knew if they had a workable relationship. They'd soon decided that they did, and now they were so loved up with their wedding plans that it was… sickening…or wonderful. Mary Jane felt both, depending on her mood.

But maybe this thing starting to happen between her and Joe wasn't that same kind of glorious love. Wasn't remotely like it, and Lee could recognize the difference.

*I can't dress as if I'm giving myself to him on a plate.*

So she deliberately chose something much safer, an outfit that she wore around the resort when she wanted to be pretty and professional but comfortable, too—a plain skirt in a soft gray that fell in nice folds around her legs and a white knit top that didn't cling too close.

Makeup, dangly earrings and heeled pumps made it all work for a more formal setting, if that was what he'd chosen. But if they went to a bar she wouldn't be overdressed.

"You look great," he said when he picked her up, meeting her out front of the office after she'd just come back from checking on everything with Daisy in the restaurant, and she had to laugh at herself for fretting over the whole issue because, really, he'd barely looked at her.

Well, not at her clothes.

He would probably have said she looked great if she'd been wearing sweats, and he would have worn that same heated, hazy look on his face. He would have done the same flicking look up and down her body that told her he was looking *through* her clothes, not at them.

It shocked her—and melted her—and she loved it… that he was prepared to show his desire for her so clearly. And maybe she was no better, because she, too, was way more aware of his body than his clothes—the dark pants, the smart polo shirt and casual jacket, and underneath all that olive-tan skin like satin over his muscles.

"Where are we going?" she asked him, wondering if Lee was watching them through the office window, and what she was thinking if she was.

"No idea," he said. "Didn't get that far."

"No?"

"Got as far as arranging things with Dad and calling you and having a shower and jumping into the car. Sorry. You were expecting something—"

"I wasn't expecting anything. I don't mind where we go. Anywhere."

He looked pleased about this. Because it let him off the hook? Or because it gave away her giddy need? "There's a waterfront place a few miles up the lake," he said. "Do you know it?"

"Yes, we have their brochure, and guests have said good things. I've never eaten there myself."

"Dad and I took the girls there for lunch when we first moved back here. Menu's nothing fancy, but the atmosphere is good, and it's a nice night. Sound okay?"

"It's fine. I really don't mind."

"Neither do I." He squeezed her suddenly. "I don't mind anything. Except this. This is great. This is wonderful."

"Yeah? Is it?" She tried to smile.

"Don't you think?" He hadn't stopped squeezing her. He was pulling her close, planting a huge kiss on her temple and another one on her hair.

She went shaky because it felt too wonderful. The casualness of it. The lack of game-playing. He was kissing her in strange places just because he wanted to, and because later they would get to the usual places, the intense places.

Was Lee watching?

Mary Jane didn't even care.

They went to the restaurant he'd talked about, overlooking the lake a little farther north, where it was quieter and less densely populated by motels and resorts and summer homes. They sat out on the open deck and ate fishermen's baskets of crumbed seafood, along with salads and fries. He had a beer and she had a glass of white wine, and then they shared a huge slice of cheesecake for dessert.

The cheesecake was crumbly and messy and very, very sexy to eat, sharing the plate, watching him scrape his teeth across his lower lip to gather in a smear of sweet, lemony cheesiness.

What did they talk about? Hard to say. It was a whole, rambling wander of a conversation about the girls and his dad and his law studies and the resort remodel and her sisters and his brothers, never touching too seriously on anything.

Not until right at the end, when they'd been talking about the girls again and he asked, "What about you? Do you like kids? You must have them up to your ears around the resort in summer, but do you want any of your own?"

He took her so much by surprise with such direct questions that all she could do was be honest about it. "Yes, I do like them. I do want them. I always have."

"Just hasn't happened? You've never been married?"

She sighed. "Short answer, Joe, is that I wasted too much time on the wrong man."

"Give me his address."

She laughed, relieved that he'd joked about it. "No need. Over it now."

"But you can't get those years back."

"No, that's right, I can't." And how needy and desperate did I sound just then? "What about you?"

"Can't get the years back, either. What, you thought I had a time machine?"

She laughed again. "No. You know what I mean! Would you want another baby—babies—if you were in another relationship?"

It was so totally and absolutely not the kind of question you were supposed to ask on a first date. She couldn't believe she'd been so blunt and upfront. But then he'd been just as direct, and he'd said it first. They both seemed to be feeling the same urgency, the same need to cut to the heart of things. She didn't want to ask herself why, in case the answer seemed too dangerous.

"I would," he was saying. "I'm daunted just thinking about it. But I definitely would. With the right woman. Because it was so wrong last time, with the girls. It's nearly killed me to get them back on track…to get *us* back on track, the three of us, as a family, and I don't think we're quite there yet. I'd like to see what being a father is like with the right foundations in place. I'd like some joy, and some sharing, at the baby and toddler stage, instead of all the hell and fear."

He stopped, and she couldn't find any words, so he helpfully pointed out to her a minute later, "You're not saying anything."

"Uh, no, I'm not."

"Does it sound weird, what I said?"

"No. It sounds…impressive."

He gave quite a shout of laughter at this. "Impressive?"

"Yes. That you would think that way. Must take courage. To want to go through it all again. Even if it was very different, the second time around."

"Courage…or craziness," he suggested.

"That, too. I've always wanted to embrace the craziness. Glad I'm not alone."

"You're not." He reached out for her hands across the table, and she met him halfway and didn't know what was happening.

Too much.

Too fast.

Too nice, all of it, and she couldn't trust that.

He squeezed her hands tight, then softened his grip and caressed her skin lightly, sending tingles up her arms and all through her body. "Should we get going?" he said softly.

She nodded.

They drove back, and when he pulled in front of the Spruce Bay office, he cut the engine at once. The office was closed and in darkness, since it was after nine-thirty. Lee would have locked it before driving up to Jay, but of course Mary Jane had a key.

She took a deep breath. "Are you coming in?"

He answered in that low voice of his, "If I'm invited."

"You're invited."

Her heart began to beat faster as soon as she'd said it. Just a handful of words between them and she was jumping in with both feet. She hadn't done this in so long. The last time had been a short-lived fling on one of her intrepid vacations, several summers ago. She'd spent her days in Turkey seeing ancient ruins and dramatic landscapes and her nights being whispered to in Danish by a lovely guy five years younger than she was, with both of them knowing there was no future in it.

It had unsettled and saddened her more than she'd expected, so she hadn't done it since. A little flirting, yes, but no sleeping together. She'd discovered that making love to a man was the key that unlocked her heart, and it felt too painful and wrong when it didn't go anywhere.

So she felt raw…and rusty…and in a kind of danger she clearly understood—and she wanted to sleep with Joe anyway.

Her hand wasn't steady as she unlocked the office and hit the lights. Joe was right behind her, touching a hand to her waist and then letting go again, closing the door with a soft click as soon as they were both inside.

He didn't wait to kiss her until they'd climbed the stairs. Instead he turned her into his arms right there by the door, and whispered in her ear, "So glad you said yes."

"So am I."

He held her, strong arms making a warm wrap for her body. "Are you shaking?" He pressed his mouth to her neck, and it made her tingle and draw in a shuddery breath.

"Probably."

"Why?"

"Because I haven't done this in a while."

"Snap."

"Really?"

"Don't."

"What?"

"Make assumptions about who I am, based on who I was."

"Okay." She couldn't if she tried, the way he was kissing her. She couldn't do anything anymore, except loll in his arms and react to what he was doing to her. Which was blissful. Mouth everywhere, whispered words of pleasure and need. Hands like heaven.

By the time they went upstairs, her legs would barely move. He went behind her, with his hand on her butt the whole way, and she liked it there. When he felt for one moment as if he might let the contact drop, she stopped so that he caught up, and leaned back into him, feeling his weight and strength and heat behind her, holding her in place. "Keep touching me. Don't stop."

"Hell, no!"

They went direct to the bedroom—the one she'd had since childhood, but had revamped a couple of times since then, to reflect her adult self. There was no nonsense about having coffee beforehand, or talking. They didn't even turn on the lights. The cream drapes were open and there was plenty of light coming in. Moonlight, and the low lighting in the resort grounds.

He peeled off his jacket and shirt, while she didn't know where to start. Shoes. Earrings. She was still fumbling with those when he reached for her again, the bare skin of his torso so hard and silky and warm and beautiful that she couldn't keep her hands away.

He slid his hands inside the waistband of her skirt to push it down, and she managed to let go of his chest and get the second earring, fiddling at it. He seemed to take this as a signal that he was supposed to do the rest, and she stood there helplessly, in a net of sensation, while he slid her top up over her head and dropped the skirt to her feet and made love to her underwear.

"It's blue," he said.

"Yes, it is."

"Been wondering what colors you liked."

"All sorts of colors."

"I like blue. And all sorts of colors."

"Take it off…please?"

"Not yet." He traced his fingers over the bra cups, instead, and she knew he must be able to feel her hardened nipples. Then he explored the lines on her backside where her panties ended and her skin began, and the whole universe narrowed just to this—that one line of flaming, erotic touch against each cheek, and then at the crease at the top of her thighs, and then the whole twin round shapes of her butt lightly squeezed in his hands. "*Now* I'll take it off," he said on a growl.

Her breath was so shuddery she couldn't reply.

He took it off *slo-o-w-ly*, starting with the straps of her bra. One, then the other. Teased from her shoulder with that knowing, whispering touch. To tackle the fastening, he turned her around and pressed his whole body against her back, which probably wasn't necessary in order to get those hooks undone. In fact it impeded and delayed the process. But she had no complaints.

The hot, rippled press of his body against her near-naked back, the ridge she could feel nestling itself in the middle of her backside through the fabric of his pants, his hands cupping her breasts from behind. Why would she complain?

Finally, he stepped back a little and reached for the hooks. The bra fell. He slid her panties down from behind, also, and she stepped out of them, then rolled around and back into his embrace. "You now, Joe."

"That's easy," he muttered, and proved the truth of this with a few quick movements.

Naked, he was…

Well, she didn't have words.

He was there.

And beautiful.

And hers—for now, at least.

They closed together again, nothing in the way, everything a mass of clean sensation. She touched his hips, the hard muscles at the backs of his thighs, the sleek shape of his spine. The dark hair on his chest pressed against her breasts, and his mouth was a long, long, delicious feast.

Finally, they arrived at the bed, peeling back the covers and falling against the cool cotton of the sheets. He lay over her, weight half on his forearms, mouth an inch from hers, the heaviness of his body warm and utterly wanted.

Crunch time.

She remembered something. "I don't have any… I mean I'm not—" She brushed the hair back from his forehead, the gesture a kind of apology for her lack of preparation.

"If you're talking about protection…"

"Yes."

"Came prepared. I put 'em on the bedside table before."

"Oh, I didn't see."

"No, you were busy… Was hoping for this from the start, you see," he said. The words were rushed and low and confessional. "Plotting it all evening."

"We both made it pretty obvious."

"I liked that."

"Me, too."

"You're amazing, Mary Jane." His eyes were so dark. It was incredible to her that they were doing this, that it was really happening. It filled her whole world, right now, and seemed to answer every bit of the yearning in her heart. "You going to amaze me, Joe?" she asked him almost shyly.

"Going to try."

He didn't have to try. It came naturally to both of them. He lavished attention on her whole body, tracing a path of fire down from her mouth to her breasts and lower. She arched her hips to meet him and almost exploded in seconds, and when he stopped to reach for the packet on the bedside table, she whimpered in loss.

He wasn't gone long, and when he came back... First thrust perfect, instantly filling her, stopping an ache she'd forgotten existed. Or maybe had never known. He made love like a musician, playing her body, making it sing and writhe, his rhythm perfect and filled with intuition about her desires.

She came first.

Helplessly.

Not expecting it yet.

It swamped her, flooded her and she cried out as it swept her away. He held on to her bucking body and anchored her safely in this world, because she might have gone into some other place if he hadn't, and never come back again.

Yes, it felt that strong.

Then it was his turn, hard on the end of her own release.

She loved that. It meant she had time for him. They had time for each other. He'd devoted himself to her, and now it was her time to give back. She widened her legs, squeezed him harder, gripped his backside and pulled him tighter against her, and he was beautiful about it. Just beautiful. She wouldn't ever have thought to describe a man that way before, but he was. A long, shuddery groan, a tightening of every muscle, her name under his breath…and finally stillness.

It felt too good to be real. She had to keep touching him to make sure it really was. She had to say his name and nestle against him and breathe in his fresh, musky smell. Just so she was really sure.

## Chapter Ten

Again, maybe?

Mary Jane was asleep right now, but Joe couldn't help wondering what would happen if he woke her up. And he couldn't help imagining how he would do it.

Sneakily, he thought.

He had his arm flung across her stomach, high enough that he could feel the nudge of her breasts. He loved that, the tease and promise of *ju-u-s-t* touching them. They were so nice. She was nice all over. Fabulous all over. Soft and responsive and—

Definitely, he'd do it sneakily. He'd begin by just brushing his forearm lightly back and forth against those two lovely weights of womanhood. Then he might use the ball of his thumb on a nipple. Or maybe softly cup his hand in her crotch and feel her begin to melt before she was even awake. He would press his mouth into her neck, which was so warm and fragrant in sleep. Her whole body was warm and fragrant.

The evening had chilled down and they were both wrapped beneath the covers. The bed smelled of her— her shampoo and soap and femaleness, all sweet and delicious. Strands of her hair tickled his face. Maybe he should start with her hair, brush it away, lean in and whisper a kiss across her lips then watch what it did to her sleeping mouth. Would she go chasing it?

So many ways to do this.

All of them good.

It had been so long!

But it was after midnight, and he should go home. He hadn't specifically said to Dad that he'd be out this late, but he'd hinted at an openended evening.

*Don't wait up, Dad. Or worry.*

All the same, one or other of the girls occasionally still woke in the night. They'd had some bad nightmares over the years, coming at unpredictable intervals, lessening as time went on but still inclined to ambush a good night's sleep occasionally.

Grandad wouldn't be the same as Dad, if Holly or Maddie was crying and still in the grip of it, fearing the Bad Man or the Bad Place. Both of these figured often in their nightmares and Joe hated to think the Bad Man and the Bad Place might be one of their mother's boyfriends and the various sordid little apartments she'd skipped out on when she owed rent.

Surely they'd been too young to remember any of that, but still he worried about it.

He needed to go home.

Mary Jane woke up when he was partway dressed, and he stopped with his hand on his fly when he saw her looking at him through the half-dark, her face scrunched against the light he'd turned on in the hallway. "Joe?"

"Sorry. The girls. They wake up sometimes, and I don't want Dad to be disturbed."

"Of course."

"I'm really sorry."

"No, of course you have to go. Give—give them a hug for me if they wake up. Or in the morning."

"I will." He wouldn't.

*Here's a hug from Mary Jane.*

He didn't want questions from them.

Not yet.

Not when he didn't know where this was going. Mary Jane had said she wanted babies, but taking on two seven-year-old kids who weren't hers was very different. The girls were part of the deal. If her interest in them didn't extend to more than casually thinking they were sweet and cute, then this relationship wouldn't get very far.

Too soon to think about that.

She lay there under the covers and watched him finish dressing, and there was a little moment where they shared a grin, because she was looking with intent, and he liked it and was embarrassed about it at the same time. It was odd how almost shy he felt. Shy and young and made new.

Weird.

Good.

"See something you like?" he couldn't help asking. It sounded brasher than the way he actually felt.

"All of it," she said.

"If I could see more of you, I'd like all of that, too."

At this, she just smiled, and it was the smile that drew him back to the bed. He lay beside her on top of the covers and buried his face in the thick, puffy comforter right at her breasts, while she tried to hug him with her arms trapped underneath. "Hell, Mary Jane," he whispered. "Can't even tell you how much more of this I want, as soon as we can."

"Yes, please," she said.

Whew! So they were clear, and they agreed, and he didn't need to know how she really felt about the girls quite yet. After all, she'd said and done all the right things so far.

The Richardsons took a break from their horses over the weekend, and gave Lucy the weekend free, also. She came into the office on Saturday morning to ask Mary Jane about the local bus service and various attractions and activities, because she wanted to explore the area like a young woman fancy-free, instead of a nanny with children in tow.

Mary Jane told her about trips up Prospect Mountain and discount passes for the theme park, and about the best bars for someone who didn't want to be hit with sleazy pickup lines all night.

A little later, Phil Richardson came in to ask about boating on the lake. Was it too late to order one of the picnic hampers from the restaurant? And could she recommend which islands they should dock at for exploring and lunch?

Technically, it *was* too late to order a picnic hamper. The deadline for those, each day, was supposed to be when the office closed the previous night. But with the Richardsons extending themselves so willingly to make the arrangement with Joe's girls work out well, Mary Jane was more than prepared to be flexible herself.

"Of course it's not too late," she told Phil. "Not for you guys, anyhow. Do you have our brochure with the options?"

"Studied it in detail already. We'd like the family basket."

"Safest option," Mary Jane agreed. "But we'll add a couple of extra adult treats, don't worry!"

"Might just grab a few more of your brochures while I'm in here."

"Go right ahead. That's what they're here for."

"Those Capelli girls are little characters, aren't they?" he said as he browsed.

She had to will the blush away from her face. Their dad was a character, too. A big, gorgeous character who wouldn't leave her mind free for much else, today—just memories from last night, and hopes for what they would plan when he called. "They are," she agreed, not daring to say much more than this.

"We're enjoying having them around. Jess and Si have grown up with horses and ponies since they were babies and take it all for granted a bit. Holly and Maddie are so wide-eyed and keen, it makes our two appreciate what they've got."

"Their dad was a little worried they might get over-excited and not behave."

"They've been fine, so far. Well, ask Lucy, of course, but she hasn't said anything to us, and Jess and Si seem to like them. They had a ball playing in the sand Thursday afternoon, apparently."

"I'm so glad," Mary Jane said. "Joe really wants it to work."

"Yes. He seems like a good bloke." Phil took his handful of brochures and left the office, flapping them in her direction as a casual goodbye.

His attitude to Joe had been casual, also, and Mary Jane felt an absurd urge to tell him more. About Joe's struggle for full custody, about the part-time law degree, about the way he'd turned his back on his star-studded ambitions and found other passions and priorities, about—

Well, everything, crazy and irrational though this was.

Her heart was melting today. Exploding. Bouncing. Full.

He called at noon, when the office was quiet and Mary Jane was catching up on the bookkeeping and bills. "I don't think we can make it work today," he said over the phone, reluctance coloring his voice. "Dad has the girls until one, when I'm closing the garage. After that, he'll need a break, but I have to put in some exam prep, so I'm parking them in front of a movie or two. If I can get four hours, I'll be happy, and after that I really need to spend some decent time with them."

"It's fine, Joe."

"Thought I'd take them for mini golf and pizza."

"I could come for mini golf and pizza, too..." She wished the words unsaid as soon as they were out.

But he jumped at them. "I was hoping you'd say that. Didn't want to come out and ask."

"You should have."

"You're right. It's nice when we're honest."

"It is. Anyhow, doesn't matter because I offered."

"You did. Do you mean it?"

"Of course I do."

So they settled the plan, and then Mary Jane remembered that Nickie had arranged for tonight off, and Lee wasn't planning on being here, either. Call back and cancel Joe?

She picked up the phone and called Lee, instead. "Can I ask a favor?"

Lee whistled again when she heard what it was.

"Lee, you really have to stop doing that."

"Doing what?"

"Whistling when I mention Joe Capelli."

"I disagree. I think whistling is entirely appropriate."

"Are you whistling because I have a date, or because it's Joe."

"Because it's Joe, mainly. And because this time last week we hadn't seen him in about seventeen years. Not surprised you have a date with him, though."

"No?"

"What single man in his thirties wouldn't want to date someone like you? You're smart, you're—"

Mary Jane cut her off. She'd heard it before. "I'd have to check the latest census data to give you a statistic on your claim. What single man? Probably several million of them." She knew what Lee's list of her attributes would have been. *Smart, funny, attractive, caring.* She'd not only heard it before—from her sisters and from the friends, married and single, that she didn't manage to catch up with often enough—she'd said it to herself a hundred times, on the days when she resolved to make only positive affirmations about herself.

*I am smart, funny, attractive, caring.*

"Listen, Mary Jane," Lee was saying, "Alex Stewart not wanting to marry you six, ten, twelve years ago makes *him* a jerk, it doesn't make *you* an unwanted harpie."

Mary Jane suppressed her usual inner cringe at one of her happily in love and pregnant younger sisters giving her the relationship pep talk. *Go, sister, go, sister, go, go, go.* They meant well. She knew they did. "I know," she said, cheery and offhand.

"Yeah, do you?"

"You haven't answered my question, Lee."

"What question was that, again?"

"Whether you can possibly staff the office this evening, so I can do the mini golf and pizza plan with Joe and his girls."

"Oh, right, sorry. Got sidetracked."

"Yes, you did."

"Let me check with Mac." She covered the phone with her hand, and Mary Jane heard some muffled sounds. The consultation didn't take long. "Yep, I can staff the office."

"You sure?"

"I was sure from the moment you asked. I would love it if you have something important happening with Joe and his girls. But I have to remember to share the decision-making with Mac now."

"Thanks, then, and thanks to Mac, too."

"No problem, Mary Jane. I'll see you at five."

So Mary Jane spent four hours on the Spruce Bay finances, while Joe spent four hours on the New York bar exam, and Lee arrived twenty minutes ahead of him to take over in the office so that Mary Jane could freshen up. His minivan swung into the parking area just as she was ready, and she raced down so that he didn't come inside because she didn't want Lee trying any helpful matchmaking activity if she and Joe came face-to-face. That could get embarrassing.

"You're out of breath," he told her when she jumped into the passenger seat.

"Ran downstairs."

"Yeah?"

"For my health."

"Right."

"Okay, truth is that I didn't want my sister raising my blood pressure."

"She can do that?"

"She can be a little blunt." She left unsaid the reasons for Lee's possible bluntness, and the girls provided a distraction from the backseat.

"We don't know which mini golf to go to, Mary Jane."

"Depends if you want splashy water or tricky holes," she answered at once.

"Nice summary," Joe said.

"Guests are always asking and that's pretty much what the choice boils down to."

There was a very atmospheric consultation in the backseat as Joe wound his way up the drive. Some whispered words, some sounds and movements that seemed to weigh the pros and cons of each option.

While this was taking place, he asked her, "Which do you personally prefer?"

"Haven't played mini golf for about six years. But it depends on my mood and the weather. Splashy water works great when it's hot."

"I think they went to one of the splashy water places with Dad. Tricky holes sound like more of a competitive challenge. And you haven't played in six years, you say…"

"Is that code for you saying you'll beat me into the ground, since I'm out of practice, if they choose tricky holes?"

"Not at all, Mary Jane." His indignant tone was very innocent. "How could you even think that?"

Finally, an announcement came in unison from the girls. "Tricky holes!"

*"E-e-x-cellent,"* Joe said in an evil voice.

He did beat her. All three of them beat her, although Maddie and Holly were permitted to cheat a little to achieve their equal second-place finish. Mary Jane didn't mind coming last. She couldn't really take the competitive element seriously at all. She was too busy thinking how sweet and fun and precious this was, how like a family they were—like all the other families playing mini golf.

Children being encouraged or growing frustrated. Moms laughing. Dads letting their kids almost beat them but not quite. Holes-in-one earned from flukish strokes. Maddening near-misses that earned groans of sympathy from the other family members watching. Amused glances exchanged by adults over the heads of the children when they did something cute. When it happened between Mary Jane and Joe, her heart beat faster every time.

*If I could have this in my life...*

She wanted it so much it hurt with a fresh, painful intensity, and she had to pull herself back, remind herself that this was only their second date, and it was only five days since she'd brought her car into Joe's garage. She had to stay in the moment, enjoy this for what it was, not keep hoping that it was a promise of things to come.

*The moment. Stay in the moment, Mary Jane.*

Holly and Maddie skipped energetically around.

"Shall I get your ball for you, Daddy?"

"Quick, it's going to roll under the fence!"

"No, it's my turn!"

"How did you get your ball to do that, Holly!"

"Can we have ice cream?"

Joe told them no, about the ice cream. "We'll have dessert after pizza, and that's enough of a sweet treat for one day, because the pizza place we're going to has huge desserts."

They were all hungry by the time they reached the eighteenth hole. The colorful balls disappeared down it one by one and didn't come back, and the girls solemnly returned their clubs, reaching up to place them on the ledge at the little kiosk out front. "But we didn't win a free game," they told the young man staffing the window.

"No? No hole in one on the volcano?" he said.

"A hole in twelve," Holly answered.

"A hole in *sixteen!*" Maddie came in, as if it was a competition for the highest number.

"A hole in twenty bazillion!" Holly shrieked.

"Sixty-five gazillion million trillion!"

"That's enough, girls!" Joe said, wincing.

Then they piled back in the minivan and headed south on Route 9N for their meal.

It was as much of a family celebration as the mini golf, and another struggle for Mary Jane. She didn't want to hold herself back from the girls, because then they might decide they didn't like her. And anyhow, it wasn't honest. Joe had said he liked the honesty between them, and she hated being cool and distant with kids.

But if she was *too* warm with them, what would Joe think? That she was auditioning to be their new mom? Trying to impress him with her maternal attributes?

Behind these questions, she could once again hear Lee and Daisy like a cheer squad.

*Go, Mary Jane! You're smart, funny, attractive, caring...*

Why did she have to analyze and second-guess everything like this?

She made a massive effort and turned off the voices of doubt in her head. The girls were absorbed in their chocolate banana splits, after their slices of leftover pizza had been boxed to take home, while she and Joe weren't having dessert but still had a glass of wine each to finish. "Want me to test you for the bar exam?" she asked him, scrambling for a topic that wasn't too personal, and one that didn't involve the girls.

"You mean now?"

"Is it a dumb idea?" She leaned over the table and twisted a little, giving her shoulder to Holly, who was seated beside her.

"No, it's not. I'm not sure that you could exactly test me, but I can talk you through some of the sample essay questions I've been doing, and you can tell me what you think of my arguments."

"Okay, shoot."

"Might be really boring."

"Pick a case that's not boring. A really juicy dispute between neighbors over encroaching tree roots, or something."

"That's not boring?"

"Depends. If it escalates into the stealing of lawn furniture and garden gnomes, I'll be on the edge of my seat."

He laughed, then said, "Well, there's a pretty nice case involving embezzlement and arson…"

"Go for it!"

His argument lasted all through the chocolate banana split, and just as the girls were beginning to get restless, he finished "…so there's a clear precedent, and that's the way I went with my argument."

"And of course I have no idea if you're right," Mary Jane said, "but you talked it through really clearly. I understood the issues, and the way you made your case."

"Good, because so much of it is how you argue. Language is an amazing thing. You can use it to make things clear, or to completely confuse and misdirect. In the law, you act as if it's factual and precise, and it can be, but it can also be so emotional and loaded, too."

"Are you practicing your exam *again,* Daddy?" said the girls, rolling their eyes.

"Have to, my honeys, or I won't pass."

"What happens if you don't pass?"

"I'll take it again until I do." He turned to Mary Jane again. "But it's interesting. The pass rate is highest for first-time takers, and for people who've done their degree in the state of New York. It drops for repeaters and for people who've studied elsewhere. I find that incredibly discouraging at three o'clock in the morning when I can't sleep."

"It's just statistics," Mary Jane said.

"I tell myself that. But you can't help reading it as a message that says, 'Pass the first time, California-law-school sucker, or you never will.'"

"Gotta avoid the negative talk, Joe," she told him, because she knew all about that.

Apparently he did, too. "So I tell the mirror every day."

"Mirror isn't impressed?"

"Not that I've noticed."

The girls needed to go home. They were still at the table, but only just. Any minute, their wriggling bodies looked as if they might ricochet all around the room.

"Can I get this?" Mary Jane asked, putting her hand over the black plastic folder with the check tucked inside it. It seemed like the safest way of saying how much she'd valued the evening.

But Joe shook his head. "No, you can't. It's mine. Those chocolate banana splits were the big-ticket item."

He was exaggerating on that, but not wanting to turn it into a big deal, Mary Jane didn't argue. At Spruce Bay, she didn't need him to tell her that this was the end of the evening. "Have to get these two home," he said. "I'd love to come back. But I'd better not."

"The bar exam?"

"How did you guess? Is that okay? Could I call you when I take a break and tell you in very nonlegal language about how much I wish I was with you and what I'd be doing if I was?"

"You could." The attempt at being coy and a little hard to get lasted about two seconds, then she added what was really in her heart. "I hope you do. Please do. I'll be here."

"I'd kiss you if the girls weren't watching," he muttered

out of their hearing. She saw his gaze drop to her mouth and it felt like a kiss—the hottest *promise* of a kiss she'd ever had. "Tomorrow," he said, making it a statement, not a question. Then he seemed to realize that it needed to be a question. "Tomorrow?"

"Depends when. I'm working most of the day."

"At night, after the girls are in bed. Just for a couple of hours. Can I come over?"

"Wait until I close the office at nine-thirty?"

"If that's what works best for you, then, yes, nine-thirty."

"See you then," she agreed.

"See you. Talk to you before that."

"Yes."

*Oh, shoot... Oh, damn... Oh, everything!*

She wanted this too much.

## Chapter Eleven

The next night, two hours unfolded into three, and unfolded some more.

Joe arrived ten minutes early, bringing dark whiskey chocolate and a cream liqueur. "Thought you might need to unwind."

"You thought right." Mary Jane rubbed the back of her neck. She'd had an evening filled with difficult guests, and reservation tangles. A couple of complaints about dishes missing in cabin kitchens, bookings canceled and remade and changed. "But I can't. Not yet."

"What's up?"

She told him.

The smoke alarm had gone off in one of the motel rooms and she couldn't get it to stop, even though there was no obvious cause. In the end, with the occupants begging her to do something about the noise, she'd disconnected it. Then they'd wanted to move rooms because of fire risk and she'd had to juggle things around and give them a room already reserved for some guests who hadn't yet shown.

The couple would probably arrive soon to check in, and this was a problem she hadn't yet solved.

"Do you have spare alarms?" Joe asked.

"I do. The guests didn't want to wait while I fitted one. They decided the room was 'unsafe' and that was that."

"Seems like an overreaction on their part, but let me put one in for the new people."

"That's the easy bit. The other couple only checked in today, but somehow they've still made a mess in the bathroom, and the bed looks used and there's dirt on the floor. So the room has to be cleaned before the new couple arrives, and of course our cleaning staff are long gone."

"C'mon, we can do it together. You'd probably better do the bed and the bathroom, but I can fit the alarm and vacuum the floor."

"No, Joe, you don't want to be—"

He pulled her into his arms and said a quarter-inch from her mouth, "Mary Jane Cherry, do I really have to tell you why I'm impatient to get it done?" The quarter-inch disappeared and she closed her eyes, and it was like their phone conversation late last night, so much power in such small details. He was right. He didn't have to tell her why.

How did he do this? How could he make her forget everything so quickly? It was a wicked kiss, so deliberate in the way it teased. He knew she couldn't move and that her legs had turned to jelly. He could tell. He could feel. He knew she'd closed her eyes because she wanted to shut out the whole world except for him.

After a few seconds, she stopped even trying to pretend. "Oh, Joe," she whispered, and pressed her mouth against his neck, tasting his skin, before she lifted her face for his kiss once more. She found all the places she wanted to touch—his work-hardened back, his tight, beautiful muscles, the hard length of his thighs, the beard-roughened shape of his jaw.

He was laughing, even while he squeezed her against him and melted against her mouth. "See? Need to be able to close up this office and switch off the ringer on the phone, don't we?"

"Mmm."

He laced his fingers in the small of her back and swung her from side to side. "So we'll clean first, and we'll do it faster if there's two of us."

"Does doing it faster with two apply to the next item on the agenda, too?"

He grinned at her. "No, it's weird that doesn't work the same way at all. The next item on the agenda goes a lot, lot slower instead."

Reluctantly, they let each other go.

She went through to the storage and supply rooms behind the office and found the box of smoke detectors and the cleaning supplies, then put the answering machine on and locked the office. On the office door, she attached the sign with the clock hands that she could adjust to show what time she'd be back, and they went over to the motel room together. It was at the end of the row of rooms, overlooking the pool and barbecue area on one side and the woodsy landscape between the cabins and cottages on the other.

It took them the full twenty minutes she'd estimated, and they were just finishing up when the phone rang in her pocket and it was the guests she was expecting. They were parked outside the unattended office, wanting to know where she was.

"Drive over to your room," she told them. "Room 20,

at the end of the north wing. I'm just checking that it's in order, and I have your keys for you here."

"What'll they think?" Joe asked. "Two of us in here, this late at night?" He had his sleeves rolled to the elbow and his top three buttons undone, and looked energetic and capable in his jeans and running shoes, with a cleaning bucket at his feet.

"Well, we have the right props," she said.

"Props? Are you suggesting a little role play, Miz Cherry?" He swooped right up to her and hauled her against him, one strong arm wrapping around her backside and swinging her weight onto his hip. Her breath huffed out and she could have swooned. He was grinning at her wickedly, daring her to play along, mouth close to hers. "The buttoned-up hotel manager and the handyman with the tool…belt…that she can't resist?"

*Okay, Joe Capelli, I can match you on this.*

"Admittedly, yes," she said to him, giving her head a sly tilt. "She's been watching those rippling muscles for weeks. Um, let's see now, you mentioned a tool belt. Ah, yes, Rod Steele—the name suits him so well, and the tool belt is mighty fine."

"Rod Steele, huh?"

"Don't you think?"

"And Rod has been watching the way Miss, uh, Miss Melody Knickers…"

"Really, Rod?"

"Really. The way Miss Melody licks her lower lip and brushes back her hair every time she sees him." He brushed the ball of his thumb across her mouth, and tucked a strand of hair behind her ear.

"And when Miss Melody has to page Rod Steele for a repair job, her heart goes all fluttery, and she's been stripping him to the buff in her fevered imagination…"

"And now, at last, they're alone, and there's a huge bed right in front of them, and they're both thinking—"

She pushed him away. "They're both thinking that the sound of the car outside is the guests arriving, because it only takes about a minute to drive over from the office, and Rod had better grab that cleaning equipment this second, because it's one of those fantasies that just wouldn't work right now."

"You are such a spoiler."

"Only now. Later I won't be."

"Promise?"

"Promise." She grinned at him and then opened the motel room door.

She welcomed the guests and told them to drop in to the office the next morning to check in properly. They were staying all week, and she had all their booking details in the computer, so there was no urgency. If the couple thought there was anything strange in her pink cheeks, and Joe's presence, and the exaggerated I-am-a-janitor way he was carrying the cleaning equipment, they didn't say so.

Ten minutes later, they were safely upstairs in her apartment, with the resort going quiet for the night and the office locked again.

She was amazing.

Joe really hadn't expected her to go for that role-play thing back in the motel room, but she'd played along with a wicked smile on her face, an even wickeder gleam in her eyes, and some impressive quick thinking when it came to the ridiculous name she'd given him.

Rod Steele.

Ridiculous, and yet strangely flattering…

He couldn't help wondering what would have happened if the guests hadn't shown up when they did. "Any chance that Rod and Melody are still around?" he asked her hope-fully once they were upstairs in the apartment.

"Nope." She smirked at him, and the gleam was back. "They've clocked off for the night. But working the late shift we have...let's see..." She picked up the chocolate box and the bottle of cream liqueur. "Ms. Bailey Irish and Mr. Jack O'Daniel Dark, a pair of sweet-toothed rodeo rid-ers with a taste for a late-night tipple."

"Oh, we do?"

She went doubtful, all of a sudden, unsure of herself. "Only if you want. Were you kidding back there in the room?"

He gathered her in his arms again—he loved doing that, just reaching for her and pulling, and finding her right up against him, giving him her weight and softness all the way up his body. How long had he known this woman? A week? Twenty years?

Both.

"Not kidding if you weren't," he told her.

He watched her mouth as he spoke, because he loved doing that, too. She always had a look on her face that said she was half-hypnotized by his gaze held so deliberately on her lips. She didn't know which way was up, and it re-flected exactly the way he felt.

How long was it since he'd told himself that he didn't have room in his life for anything like this? About three days? The warnings he'd given himself didn't seem to mat-ter anymore. She was terrific, in bed and out of it. So far, things seemed pretty good between her and the girls. No danger signals that he'd picked up on yet. He would *make* room in his life. For once, he was going to make love to a woman who had the power to save him, instead of the capacity to destroy.

"Whatever you like, Ms. Irish," he said very soft and very low.

"I think I like what you like, Jack." She had the open box of chocolates in her hand, and she took one out and pressed it to his mouth.

He bit half, then nudged the rest between her parted lips. "I'm starting to think you might be right."

It was sweet and messy and chocolatey and slightly whiskey-flavored, with the occasional flirty slice of cowboy and rodeo queen in the mix. And it was passionate and intense and bone-melting. He'd told her two hours, but neither of them could hold to that. After two hours, they were just getting started.

Again.

Without the liqueurs and chocolate and role-play this time, just the two of them, Joe and Mary Jane, naked in her queen-sized bed, discovering each other. She loved the attention he lavished on her breasts. She hated when he accidentally tickled her sides. She loved being on top. And underneath. He loved pretty much everything.

And he very definitely didn't want to go home, not even when they were fully sated and should really be ready to fall asleep. This seemed too important, too nice, for sleep.

They lay there talking instead, spooned against each other beneath the covers.

"Is it your dad who'll be worried if you're not home, or the girls, or you?" Mary Jane asked.

"All of us." He added more truthfully, "Me, mostly. Worried that they'll be worried. Or that the girls will have a bad dream."

He told her about the dreams, and his fears about their origins.

"All kids have bad dreams," she said.

He thought that was too easy. "About bad men, and bad places?"

"I used to. Even though there was nothing in my real life to act as a source."

"So where do those things come from?"

"Scary books and movies. The dark. The underneath of the bed. Primal instinct from long ago."

"I suppose you're right."

"Maybe you worry about them too much."

Again, it sounded too easy. "I'm the only one to do it."

"I bet your dad worries, too."

"That's why I worry more, so that he can worry less."

She laughed gently, and he felt it against his stomach. He was lying behind her, arm thrown over her, cupping a sweet, soft breast in his hand. "Joe, I don't think worrying is like stacking firewood—the more you do of it, the less there is left of the job for someone else."

"You don't believe in productive, preemptive worry?"

"You'll have to explain that."

"If I worry about the right things, I can head them off before they happen, so that Dad doesn't even need to think about them."

"You mean, say, if you get to the girls when they have a nightmare, before your dad even wakes up…"

"Exactly."

"Wouldn't it be less of a burden on you, if you had someone else to share the worrying?"

"Not if that someone else is Dad. It's too hard on him."

"A different someone else? A teacher, or counselor?"

"They've had some therapy in California. I took them to someone. She was really good. Just play therapy, where she asked questions occasionally, so that if there was something on their minds they could talk about it."

"Did anything come up?"

"A few things."

"Wanna tell me?"

Yes, he did. This was good for him, he thought. He had a sense of his burdens lightening. When she'd said "Someone else?" he'd almost said, "Yes, you." But he'd clawed the words back, not wanting to scare her, not wanting to jump too far, too fast, out of...

Out of loneliness. Out of the struggle. Out of this glorious sense of rightness about lying here with her, talking about the girls and feeling increasingly reassured that she cared.

"They did a few things with dolls. Stories they acted out. The little doll couldn't get the mommy doll to wake up. She wet her pants and then the mommy doll smacked her. The superhero doll was a bad guy, not a good guy. He had a mean laugh, and he hit one of the other dolls with his gun."

She hissed in a breath, then said, "Hit, not shot?"

"Hit. Pistol-whipped. *Bam, bam, bam,* on the side of the doll's head. The therapist asked them about both those bits of play and it did seem as if they were coming from real experience. She thought they were great kids, though, couldn't see any serious signs of damage."

"So it's okay."

"That's what I tell myself."

"And you worry anyhow."

"I do."

After a moment, she told him, "Roll over."

"Yeah?"

"My turn to spoon you, now."

"Mmm, yes please..." He rolled over, and so did she, reversing their positions. She was holding now, and he was held. Held warm and strong and soft, while her lips nuzzled the back of his neck and the dip between his shoulder blades.

He knew why she was doing this. She wanted to hold him and cradle him and make everything better, and she probably had no idea how well it worked. This was what he needed.

All he needed.

Someone to care. Someone to listen, and talk him down from the ledge when his fears for the girls ballooned out of control for no apparent reason.

Was she right? Did he worry so much because he'd never really had anyone to share the worry with?

*Let me share it with you, Mary Jane.*

He had a rush of intuition so powerful it almost made him groan out loud.

This woman belonged in his life. He hadn't known her long. Not really. High school didn't count.

And yet at the same time, it *did* count. He felt as if it did. Their whole shared background counted. Her family had been bringing their cars to Dad ever since he could remember. He'd driven past the pretty painted wooden sign at the top of Spruce Bay Resort's driveway more times than he knew.

He remembered her smart, diligent presence in high school classrooms. She'd done her reading and spoke out with intelligence in class, while he'd hammed it up in the back row, caring more about getting a laugh from his friends than about actually passing the course.

She'd been a member of all the clubs, not taking on the high-profile roles but working in the background, keeping everything smooth, hosing down conflict and cliques and bullying. He remembered her receiving all sorts of awards for leadership and teamwork and community service.

No wonder he trusted her. She'd earned that trust nearly

twenty years ago, when neither of them could have recognized the fact, because his trust of women wasn't something he valued back then. He'd trusted his mom, of course. But she was just Mom. Girls weren't people to trust, they were for going after with his own very narrow agenda.

Thank the lord he'd grown up since then!

His heart felt full to bursting, and his mind was racing while she grew sleepier as she lay behind him, cradling his body against her soft stomach and breasts.

*Don't blow this, Joe. Keep seeing her. Be good to her. See where it goes. Find out if the girls like her. Find out what she really thinks about them.*

This afternoon he'd told her two hours, but ended up staying for seven. In the end, at almost four-thirty after they'd slept awhile, he only dragged himself out of her bed because of Dad and the girls, and he spent the whole drive home trying to find ways to shoehorn more time with Mary Jane into his life without dropping any of the balls he'd been desperately juggling for so long.

Mary Jane missed Joe horribly when he left.

Missed him physically, like an ache, or like being without a coat in a bitter wind. She knew he had to go home. She'd fallen asleep somewhere around two, and a couple of hours later he'd woken her gently, leaning down from a standing position beside the bed and already fully dressed. "Didn't want to just disappear while you were asleep. Really have to go."

"I know. That's fine," she told him sleepily.

"Just lock the door behind me, downstairs?"

"Yes, or do you want me to come down?"

"No. Stay."

"Okay."

"Night. Sweet dreams. See you as soon as I can."

"Hope so." She watched his shadowy figure move through the room and out the open bedroom door, then listened to him going downstairs, the rhythm of his feet hurried, as if shaving thirty seconds off his journey from her room to the car would make up for him being about five hours later getting home than he'd planned.

Before she even heard the sound of his car, the missing him started. The bed felt colder, and the doubts kicked in.

She *shouldn't* miss him so much. It was dangerous, made her vulnerable. This was all happening too fast, leaving her no time to catch her breath or keep herself safe. And no time to work out what was reality and what was the fantasy she'd wanted for so long.

Sleep refused to return, and the yearning in her felt like coiled ropes around her body. When the alarm went off at six-thirty, she knew she'd barely dozed since he left, and yet all she could think of were his last words. "See you as soon as I can."

She waited all day for him to call.

And he did, that night at seven when she'd just gotten back to the office after several hours of trouble-shooting various problems around the resort. She was tired and irritable and she knew it, but as soon as she heard his voice, any intention to have a sensible early night vanished at once.

"How're you doing?" he said, dropping his voice to an intimate pitch that made the strength drain from her limbs. Oh, that was such a cliché, but it was true! If she hadn't been sitting at the desk, she would have sagged against it.

"Good," she said, struggling to breathe right. "How about you?"

"Was good. Until I realized there's no way I can see you till Wednesday."

"Oh."

"Yeah, I know. But I *have* to study. If I don't make time for that…"

"Of course. You don't have to explain."

Or was he making excuses already?

"How about you?" he asked. "Can you do Wednesday? Same as last night? Late, for a few hours."

"Y-yes, I think so."

"And then maybe you could come over Thursday evening, just for a family dinner with Dad and me and the girls?"

"Um, as long as Nickie can do the evening in the office."

"If you don't want to…"

"No, I do."

"Let me know about it, then, when you can."

"I will."

"Can't wait."

She took a breath and went for the same honesty. "Me, neither, Joe."

## Chapter Twelve

Joe delivered the girls to the Richardsons' cottage on schedule on Friday morning, for their seventh full day of pony camp, then headed back into town to open up the garage, congratulating himself for having lucked into such a perfect arrangement.

Maddie and Holly were having the time of their lives with ponies and new friends. They often talked about Mary Jane and how they'd seen her at the resort, and she'd brought out special pool toys for them or given them a snack. They thought the only place in the world better than Penelope's horse farm was Spruce Bay.

On top of this, Dad was getting a break, Joe's share of Lucy's wages wasn't breaking the bank and he thought he'd be able to grab some study time in the garage office today if he was lucky, because he only had a few vehicles booked in.

And if he managed enough study time, he would call

Mary Jane and see if they could meet up tonight. In bed or out of it, he really didn't care. Although some of both would be very, very nice....

Wednesday night with Mary Jane had been glorious, and Thursday dinner with the family as good, although very different. She was terrific with the girls, not too gushy and not afraid to be firm with them when they needed it, but warm and genuine. She never brushed them aside, or made him feel that she was only putting on a show for his sake.

If this had been an audition, she would have moved to the very top of the callback list.

It *was* an audition, in many ways. Maybe he shouldn't be thinking of it that way, but he didn't know what else to do. The girls were as much of a test for Mary Jane as his impending bar exam was for him, and Mary Jane passing that test was even more important than him passing the bar.

*She's passing, Joe. Don't worry about it.*

Dad had been out Thursday evening, catching up over a beer and a bar meal with some old buddies, so it was just the four of them, and if this was part of the test—how they performed together as a family—they'd all passed with flying colors, not just Mary Jane.

For once in his life, Joe felt as if he might be getting something right from the word *go,* instead of making a bucket-load of horrible mistakes that took him years to claw his way back from.

The congratulatory feeling lasted until four minutes past eleven on Friday morning, when the phone call came.

"Mr. Capelli?" It was Nanny Lucy on the other end of the line. "There's been a problem here, I'm afraid." She sounded very much on edge, and a little shaky.

His heart lurched and began to pound at once.

*The girls!*

"Everything's fine. I mean, the girls are fine. But you need to come right away, if you possibly can. Penelope wants to speak to you."

"What's happened? You said they're fine."

"There was an incident."

"An *incident?*" *What the hell?*

"Are you able to come?"

"Yes. Well, ten minutes?" He'd have to grab Dad, who was probably napping. There were clients due to pick up the cars Joe had just finished working on. "But can't you explain on the—"

"Better wait until you can talk to Penelope."

*Shoot!* What parent had any patience after being told something like that?

He ended the call quickly, since Lucy clearly wasn't going to give him any detail, and immediately called his father. Dad didn't pick up. He tried again, same result. Edgy as a caged animal, he closed up the garage and jumped in the car, drove home pushing the speed limit and screeched up the driveway. Dad's car was here, so…

"Must have been asleep" was his father's explanation, after Joe had let himself in the back door and gone through the house calling for him.

"You didn't hear the phone? I called twice."

"Had the bedroom door shut. But what's up, son?"

He explained as quickly as he could, playing it down so as not to worry a doting grandfather, but of course that didn't work. Dad only had more questions—ones that Joe couldn't answer because Lucy had told him so little.

"Just an incident, she said, and that the girls are fine, but Penelope wants to speak to me. That's seriously all I know, Dad, so that's why I need to drop you at the garage while I go up there and see what the problem is."

"I'll get my shoes and socks on."

He was slow about it. He'd become perceptibly slower at those kinds of things since Joe had moved back here, compared to how he'd been during his last visit. Joe had to swallow words of impatience that wouldn't have quickened Dad's pace.

The girls were fine. That was all that mattered.

He kept telling himself this but it didn't help, because clearly not everything was fine, and all his fears came rushing into their familiar home in his heart. He never managed to keep those fears at bay for that long, remembering the girls' mother and their messed-up first few years.

He thought again about Mary Jane and the times they'd spent together this past week. Not the sex, although that had been amazing, but the way they'd dozed in bed afterward until he'd roused himself enough to dress and come home, or the way they'd talked and laughed…and kissed… in the kitchen, making dinner, while the girls played in the next room.

He remembered how she'd fitted so warm and perfect against him in bed, how good she'd smelled all the time, how happy she'd seemed in his company, and how she didn't try to hide it. He guessed she never played those kinds of games, and he loved her for that.

Could he call her? Would it help to have her with him for the "talk" with Penelope?

He wanted to, hugely, as soon as he thought of the idea, but didn't know what Penelope would think. Mary Jane had made the initial connection between them, yes, but Maddie and Holly were his, and whatever they'd done—he was already sure that they must have done something— he had to sort it out and take responsibility. Despite last night's impressive audition, Mary Jane wasn't a part of his family yet.

Dad was finally ready, making sure he had keys and wallet and handkerchief…and driving Joe slowly, inexorably crazy in the process.

*C'mon, Dad!*

He dropped him at the garage, then tore along the lake and up the hill, and Penelope was waiting for him. No sign of Lucy, Jessica, Simon or the girls.

He had to ask. "Where are they?"

"Lucy's taken them back to the motel."

"What happened?"

"I'm afraid there was an incident."

He wanted to yell his impatience, but managed to speak calmly. Cheerfully, even. "Yes, so Lucy said, but she wouldn't tell me what it was."

Penelope took a deep breath. "First, I have to tell you that I do hold myself responsible."

"You were there?"

"No, but it's my property, and ultimately that means I'm to blame."

"For what? Please…"

"Yes." She seemed to realize how crazy this was making him, and launched into the story. "Maddie forgot her helmet in the tack room after morning tea, when they were about to ride. Lucy sent her and Holly back there together to find it, telling them—as I have told them more than once—not to do anything but bring the helmet. On the way back, the girls passed one of the day yards where my stallion, Glengarlow Breve, is kept."

Joe heard the word *stallion* and every muscle in his body went tight.

"He'd knocked over his feed bucket," Penelope was saying, "and the girls decided to go in there and set it right for him."

"What happened?" He began to sweat. "You said they're fine..."

"They are fine. Nothing happened. Lucy thought they'd been gone too long and went to check on them. She found them just as they'd righted the bucket and stepped back. She had them out of there at once, with no damage done, but they were very, very lucky that Glen didn't bite or kick because he's extremely possessive about his food and he wouldn't have understood that they were trying to help him. He could have done some serious damage."

"So that's...a lot better than it could have been." He felt shaky, though.

The girls were fine. The girls were *fine*.

Penelope seemed a little shaky, too. "It is, but the point is, they'd been told quite clearly that all they were to do was bring the helmet, and they've been told several times that they are never, ever to go into any of the yards or stables or fields without express permission and without an adult with them. I can't have it, Joe. I'll be having nightmares, as it is, about what would have happened if Glen had lashed out."

He knew what was coming, and said it for her. "So this is the end of pony camp?"

"I'm afraid so." She sounded reluctant about it, disappointed at having to break the news.

It was nothing compared to what Joe felt. For a moment, he didn't trust his voice to speak, and when he finally did, it wasn't what he'd planned to say.

*Please give them another chance. They won't do it again.*

"Where were you when this was happening?" he asked scratchily instead.

"Vanessa and Phil and I were out doing some cross-country training with their eventing horses. The jumps are on a part of the property you haven't seen, in the woods, out of sight of any of the buildings. Joe, I've already told you that I blame myself. Telling the girls not to go near to my horses wasn't enough. I should have made sure of it by not ever having them out of an adult's sight. They're only seven, younger than the children I mostly have here. I do know that. But this has spooked me, and I feel I was too hasty in agreeing to the arrangement in the beginning."

"I understand."

"I have to be able to trust children to do exactly as they're told, because there are too many ways to get into trouble around horses if they decide to use their own initiative."

"Yes, so I realize."

*Give them another chance.*

"Mary Jane is a terrific woman, and all my clients are always very happy with their stay at Spruce Bay. When she approached me about this…"

"It's not her fault."

"No, absolutely not."

"Thanks for giving it a try."

"I'm sorry. I should perhaps have considered the issues for longer before I said yes."

"No, I get it. I'm just glad the girls are safe."

"They're lovely little riders, very eager to learn, lovely girls. Just a little too enthusiastic for their own good."

"Thanks. Yeah, I know about the enthusiasm."

There wasn't a lot more to say. He left shortly afterward, with Penelope reiterating her regret, her acceptance of blame and her conviction that the pony camp arrangement had to end.

Halfway down the hill, he pulled over to get himself together and think about what he needed to do next.

Pick up the girls. First item on the list.

He couldn't leave them in Lucy's care when the whole arrangement had fallen apart. He didn't know where Vanessa and Phil were, but had vaguely noticed some dust kicking up from the open-air dressage arena behind the barn, so maybe that had been them, working their horses. Or maybe they were still out doing the cross-country jumps.

A few minutes later, he drove down the resort driveway in bright noon sunshine, remembering how very differently he'd felt driving down it Monday night and Wednesday night in the dark. All that juicy-sweet anticipation about seeing Mary Jane, compared with this. Breaking the bad news to the girls, dealing with no doubt quite a large degree of awkwardness between himself, the Richardsons and Lucy.

Did Lucy feel to blame, also?

He didn't know where to park. Down in front of the Richardsons' cottage?

He wasn't ready for it yet. He just wasn't. Seeing the girls' faces, confused about why he was here. Had Penelope spoken to them at all? Had Lucy? Did they know they were in trouble? Did they have any idea what they'd done, or what could have happened?

No, he needed more time to think.

Needed someone to talk to.

Needed Mary Jane.

He parked in front of the office, and when she saw him through the window her face lit up.

What was Joe doing here, in the middle of the day?

They hadn't made an arrangement to see each other today, although he'd been hopeful last night that they might manage something. Mary Jane knew how hard it was for him, and had been imagining him at the garage, snatching time for bar exam study, running legal case studies in his head while he lay under an engine, covered in sweat and grease.

What was he doing here, instead?

Well, clearly he'd come to see her!

She opened the door to greet him, and couldn't keep the silly grin off her face and didn't even really try. "Hi…"

But he was frowning and tense and unhappy, holding himself very tight, not doing that loose-limbed, openly seductive reach for her that she loved.

"What's up, Joe?" She was the one to reach, gripping his hands and squeezing them. He squeezed back, but then tore away, too restless and distracted for body contact.

"Pony camp is off."

"What? But the girls are with Lucy and Jess and Simon right now, I saw them down at the lake beach when I was checking the boats."

"I've just come from Penelope's to pick them up."

"What happened?" She could see he felt wretched about it, whatever it was. "Tell me!"

"Penelope's stallion knocked over his feed bucket and Maddie and Holly went into his day yard and set it the right way up for him, and nothing happened but apparently he could easily have kicked if they'd put themselves between him and his food. They could have been badly hurt. Penelope says she can't have them there if they're not going to do exactly as they're told."

"Where was she when this happened?"

"She's accepting blame on that. Says she should have made it clear to Lucy that none of the kids were ever to be out of adult sight. She's not really expelling them, as such, just saying she can't handle the risk, can't risk it again."

"Well, it certainly sounds like she's expelling them!"

He looked at her sideways. "I thought you liked Penelope."

"I do like her. I like you better. And—and the girls. I understand…" What did she understand? Their hard start? His painful love?

All of it, she thought.

Had he tried to explain any of that to Penelope?

Of course not. She knew he wouldn't have. "We can fix this, Joe." Again, she tried to reach for him and he briefly responded—a trail of his hand across her back, this time—before pulling away.

"Didn't sound that way," he said. "She seemed pretty definite about it."

"I can't bear to think of them being so disappointed when they've been loving it so much, and they've tried so hard."

"Neither can I. They lasted, what, six and a half days?" There was a bitterness to the words that seemed out of proportion, and she suddenly heard them in another context. Was this what he'd said to their mother about her attempts to beat her addictions?

*You said you were kicking it, and you lasted, what, six and a half days?*

It wasn't the same situation, but to him maybe it felt that way.

"So can I please talk to her before you say anything to them?" she begged. "Or to Vanessa and Phil and Lucy."

"Lucy must know something's up. She was the one who found the girls in with the stallion." He swore. "I'm so glad they're okay. Could have been so much worse. Keep telling myself that."

"I'm going to talk to her."

He stepped back and looked at her. "I don't think you should."

"Why? I care about you so much, Joe, and I know how much you want the girls to be happy."

"I know that, but…" His face softened and scrunched up, and he seemed not to know how to continue.

And suddenly this was about how she felt, not about the girls. "Do you? Know it?"

"Hell, yes!" His dark eyes blazed.

"Good. I wouldn't have slept with you if I hadn't cared."

"I really, really know it. I do." He stopped for a moment, then continued on a rush, "It feels amazing, Mary Jane, I have to tell you. The way you've given yourself to me, the way you've understood so much."

"Why do you think it would be so hard for me to give?" She smiled at him, shy and happy. "Don't you think you're pretty easy to love?"

She hadn't meant to say that word. *Love.* It was too strong, too full of strings and complications and baggage, and she wasn't ready for it yet. But the word *like* was too weak, far too weak.

Shoot, why had she said it, though?

Joe didn't seem to mind. His attention had caught on it, the same way it seemed to catch on the shape of her mouth, all those times he acted as if he couldn't look away.

Right now, he couldn't look away from the *L* word.

"You mean that?"

"Y-yes." She couldn't back down from it, because it wasn't *not* true—if that made any sense. She didn't *not* love him, so did that mean she— "I do," she told him, taking her courage in hand. "I mean it."

She meant it.

Joe's head was spinning. He'd come to her out of blind need just now, not knowing what he would say or whether she had any power to help, but somehow she'd done it.

She'd said she loved him, and suddenly it all seemed so clear and simple.

It made sense of the past ten days, of how fast their feelings had moved, of how right everything had been, of how good she seemed to be with the girls.

"Then let's get married," he said.

*"I beg your pardon?"*

Okay, so he hadn't planned to say it. Not five minutes ago. Not even a minute. The words had formed as fast as the thought. Did that matter?

He repeated it, so she would know he meant it, coming close and reaching for her, looking down into her face. Her eyes were huge. "Marry me. I mean it. We're thirty-five. We know what *doesn't* work, and who *isn't* right. We've had the most amazing ten days together, and we've known each other since our teens. We know what we want when we see it, by this point. We know each other's background. We know all that's important."

"Do we?" She was frowning and uncertain, lashes masking those beautiful eyes now.

He didn't understand her sudden doubt. "It doesn't take long. Don't you think? You just *know*." How did you even put it into words? What did you say? "You're beautiful, and we get on, it's been so damned hard doing everything on my own, and the girls would love you for a mom." He wrapped his arms around her and tried to pull her closer, but she didn't respond. Or she half responded, feeling stiff and hesitant.

His certainty flickered, suddenly.

What had he said? Was it the girls? She hadn't given him an answer yet, but he knew what it would be before the words came, and it hit him harder than he would have thought possible.

"No, Joe," she said.

"No?" He looked down at her again, filled with a pained disbelief that seemed to distress her, even though she could have relieved it so easily with just one word.

"No, I won't marry you. I can't. I'm sorry. Not like this."

"You said you loved me. I feel the same. And I think it's for the right reasons. I honestly do."

"There's more to it than just that. We're talking about joining lives. And not just ours, but Holly's and Maddie's, too."

So it was the girls, then?

This shocked him. "I thought you loved the girls."

"I—I do. I think I do. But I've known them ten days. You're asking me to be their mother."

"And you're saying you can't."

"I'm saying…" She pressed her lips together. "I'm saying it's too soon. I'm saying I'm not sure that they are the right reasons."

"The girls aren't?"

"No…no, not that." Her distress made it hard for him to navigate the difficult conversation and his own powerful feelings at the same time.

He combed his mind for signs. The other night when they'd all had pizza, she'd turned her shoulder to Holly while the girls were having dessert, and had talked to him about the bar exam, instead, as if she wanted an adult conversation. Should he have read more into that? She'd said she wanted babies of her own, but hadn't talked about taking on another woman's children. Was her warmth and love less generous than he'd thought?

And yet she was *distressed* right now. He could see it, feel it. He wanted to push her, but his own thought of a few days ago kept coming back to her.

The girls were a deal-breaker.

They just were.

Beyond anything. Beyond compatibility in bed, and shared goals, and humor and warmth and a background they both knew, the girls were the one thing he couldn't kid himself about, couldn't leave to chance.

"I can't say yes. I just can't," she was saying.

"Okay," he answered, because it was the only word he could think of.

"I'm not…dismissing you, Joe." She laid a hand on his arm and he made a twisting movement so he could stroke his fingers down her skin, because his heart responded to her aura of unhappiness, even when he was trying to end this, find a way to leave. If she really was saying she had doubts about the girls…

"Not dismissing me, just turning me down," he said softly, seeking answers she didn't seem to want to give.

"I'm trying to protect myself. And you. And the girls. This is wrong. Too soon. All for the wrong reasons. In both of us."

This made him rebel. "Don't you think I know what I want? Don't you think I've been through enough crap in life to have a pretty good idea when I get to the gold? I know what I want, Mary Jane."

"Do you? Really?"

"Either you know or you don't."

"Then…I'd have to say I don't." But she was standing so close to him. He had to think that she was a lot more confused than she was saying.

Maybe he needed to hear her say it straight out.

*I love you, Joe, but I can't take on the girls.*

"Tell me…" he invited her softly, hoping against hope that she'd say something different, something that wouldn't end this once and for all.

"Sometimes it's really dangerous to know what you

want," she said. "You can make hideous mistakes, trying too hard to get it."

It didn't make sense. He didn't understand. But her intent was plain. He let her go. "You mean this, don't you?"

"I—I do. I think you'll understand, later, when you really think about it."

"Okay." Again, it was all he could say. He gathered himself. "Uh, I need to get the girls, break the news."

For a moment she looked confused, then her face cleared. "Oh, about pony camp."

*Yes, Mary Jane, not about you turning me down when I asked you to marry me.*

"You'd better," she said. "But I will talk to Penelope and the Richardsons, and see if there's—"

"No. Please. You don't have to do that. It's not your problem."

Especially not now.

How final was it when a woman rejected your proposal of marriage?

Pretty final, he had to think.

Joe left awkwardly. They didn't touch or kiss or talk about seeing each other again. Mary Jane guessed they weren't doing that. People tended not to, when a man had proposed marriage and the woman had turned him down.

Mary Jane's mind reeled after he'd gone, and the breath stuck in her lungs.

It was what she'd wanted for so long. All she'd ever wanted, a husband and family, the chance to make a loving home, and Joe had just offered it to her, most of it ready-made. He'd said it as if it was obvious.

*"Marry me."*

As if it was as easy as buying a new toaster, or choosing dessert, and at the same time as momentous as winning the lottery or moving to France.

With every beat of her heart, every nerve-ending, every dream-filled, yearning part of her, she'd wanted to say yes the moment she heard the words.

*Yes, yes, yes.*

She could have said it and then she would have been able to start planning a wedding right now, and dreaming of babies. They could have stopped using protection the next time they made love and she might have been pregnant before Daisy and Lee had their babies. It would have meant she could have shared their joy with none of the inner envious misery she feared she might not be able to hide from her sisters when the time came. She'd been struggling enough with their glowing pregnancies. The babies themselves would be much harder.

*Marry me.*

Hearing him ask her that age-old question had felt like crossing the finish line in a race that had lasted her whole adult life—a race she'd thought she would never finish, let alone win. It felt like winning.

Like a prize.

Like greedily snatching up the winning balls right out of the lottery machine and breathing a sigh of relief because you'd done it, you'd arrived, you were there.

But she hadn't believed in any of it, not really.

He'd said it too soon and too easily. It *couldn't* be that fast or simple. She would have been crazy to trust it, and she had too firm a hold on herself at this point in her life to do that. He'd said it because of what had happened this morning with the girls. He'd felt desperate and alone and emotional and fragile in a way that was very male.

He'd even said it. *The girls would love you for a mom... It's been so damned hard doing everything on my own.*

And so he'd grabbed at the nearest safety net, the nearest nurturing woman who'd make a good mother for his girls, and it happened to be her.

If she'd said yes, she would have done it for all the wrong reasons, just as he'd asked her for all the wrong reasons.

If she'd said yes, she would have despised herself for her own neediness and desperation. For jumping at an offer he wouldn't be making in the first place if he wasn't pretty desperate himself. For grabbing so greedily at the chance to be an instant mom. For thinking she could step into the ready-made fantasy of his life, and turn a crush and a few talks and some great moments in bed into a full-on commitment.

So she'd done the only thing possible. She'd turned him down, turned away from her dream life, and it might kill her yet.

## Chapter Thirteen

"You must understand my position, Mary Jane."

"I do, Penelope, but if the right systems are put in place...I presume Lucy very rarely let the girls out of her sight before the incident, so for you to make it clear to everyone that they're *never* to be out of an adult's sight isn't such a big change, is it? You have said that you blame yourself..."

"I wonder if I should try to run programs for children at all. It's not my central mission statement, after all. It's just something I like to do."

"Something you believe in."

Penelope sighed. "Yes. Unfortunately. I let myself in for a lot of hard work because of it!"

They were standing by the wash-bay and hitching rails. The stallion's saddle and saddlecloth sat on the top metal rail, because Penelope had just finished riding him. Glengarlow Breve was embroidered on the saddlecloth, but she always called him Glen. He was magnificent and scary, all glossy black and massively muscled and toweringly tall, with a thick mane and tail, and Mary Jane secretly thought that Maddie and Holly had been incredibly brave—and, yes, very foolish—to go anywhere near him.

After Joe had left Spruce Bay, several hours ago, Mary Jane had sat back down at the desk, checked the reservations on the website out of habit and seen that a new one had come in for September, a weeklong stay just after Labor Day. Nice, she'd thought. Their season was extending, thanks to the revamp of the resort. Great. Wonderful.

But she hadn't been able to care about the success of the resort at that moment. Not really. Most of her attention had been fixed on the resort driveway, waiting to see Joe's minivan leaving, with two miserable little skinny, dark-haired peas in a pod on board.

It had taken a full half hour to appear, so she'd guessed there had been more than one tough conversation, over at the Richardsons' cottage, and many tears to dry.

Nickie had been taking over in the office at four today, so as soon as Joe's minivan had disappeared, Mary Jane had gathered her resolve, picked up the phone and arranged to meet Penelope here at her property for a talk now, at four-fifteen, so she could go into bat for a man she wasn't going to marry and two little girls she didn't have the right to love.

So far, it was going about as well as the whole day had done up to this point.

In other words, not very well at all.

"I would hate to see you question your whole philosophy over this one incident," Mary Jane said carefully. "Hasn't anything like this ever happened before, when you've run camps?"

"We had a ten-year-old boy once, who didn't want to

be here." Penelope spoke with some reluctance. "He was referred by the county's children's services department because they thought it might be good for him, but he deliberately teased the horses. Worse. I caught him sticking nails into an apple. He thought it was funny."

Glen snorted and tossed his head and loudly pawed the concrete under his metal hoof, as if he didn't agree, because apples were way too important to be funny, with or without nails. Penelope told him firmly to stop it. He listened and stood still again, so she stroked his satiny black nose and told him, "That's right, you remember that boy, don't you, my lad?"

"What happened?" Mary Jane asked. "I presume he didn't stay on."

"He didn't. After half a day, I phoned children's services and told them I couldn't have him, and that he needed to be collected right away. I just didn't have the resources to give him the one-to-one attention he needed."

"Holly and Maddie are very, very different, though, Penelope. They adore ponies. Joe has been reading horse-care books to them for a couple of years, he told me, and they hang on every word. This whole thing with Glen happened because they wanted him to have his food. They cared about his well-being. With the boy you're talking about, it was the opposite."

"That's true." Penelope turned away from Glen's beautiful nose and gave her a penetrating look. "You're arguing this very strenuously, Mary Jane."

She heated up. "I—I care about them."

Another look. "And their father?"

"I care about him, too."

"Congratulations! How lovely!"

"No… No. It's nothing like that." Although Penelope couldn't be blamed for getting the wrong idea. Mary Jane had said the words like a confession of love. "He's just… a friend."

Now, after what had happened in the office, he was just a friend.

If that.

"Does he know you're here?"

"No. He told me to leave it alone. But I couldn't. For all their sakes."

"Are the girls upset?"

"Oh, Penelope, you know they would be! I haven't seen them, but it doesn't take much to imagine. They had a difficult time in their early years."

Should she say this?

Now that she'd started it was hard to stop. And anyhow, wasn't it why Joe had told her the girls' story in the first place, a week ago?

"They have no contact with their mother at all, now," she explained, "but Joe had a long battle to gain sole custody. She relapsed into serious addiction problems and it spiraled down and they were abused by a couple of her boyfriends before he could manage to keep them safe. They could easily have turned out like your children's services boy. Damaged. Ticking time-bombs. Joe blames himself…"

"Yes, I know how that feels!"

"And he's desperate to heal them from any legacy of that time, and I think this'll hurt the girls the most now, because they're kids and it's fresh, but in the long run it's Joe who'll be hurt the worst. He's desperate for a healthy outlet for them, a passion that can harness their energy."

"And we mustn't hurt Joe," Penelope said softly.

Mary Jane flushed even darker. "No. We mustn't. Please?"

"Somehow I don't think you're just friends."

"I don't know what we are. If you're saying I love him, then, yes, I do. I can't stop myself."

"To the point where you'd risk really, really annoying me by arguing the girls' case."

"To that point and beyond. You might never send another rider to Spruce Bay again," she tried to joke.

"Relax. You haven't annoyed me that much! Or at all, really. I needed to talk it out a little more. Probably reacted too hastily this morning. I was remembering the boy, thinking what might have happened if he'd been more subtle in his cruelty and we hadn't picked up on it in time. He could have killed one of my beautiful horses."

"I'm shuddering, too."

"But you're right. Holly and Maddie are different, and if I'm going to run these things, especially for kids in need, I do need to have a strict policy on adult supervision. I do have one, in fact, when I run the camps. Because this was a less formal arrangement, and because Jess and Si are so used to being around horses, and so clear on what they're allowed to do and what they're not, we all dropped the ball a little on Joe's girls."

"They'll get a second chance?"

"One chance. Only for you, Mary Jane. They really do need to know that it's just one chance. They cannot do anything like this ever again."

"Thank you so much! One is all they'll need, I'm sure of it. Thank you! That's better than I dared to hope."

"I'll talk to Lucy and Vanessa and Phil. You talk to Joe and the girls. But please make it clear—"

"I'll make it transparently clear. One chance. Iron-clad rules."

"You okay with that, Glenny-boy?" Penelope crooned to the horse.

"Does he have a say in it? They won't be going any-where near him!"

"You're right." She gave a chuckle. "They certainly won't."


Mary Jane.

What was she doing here?

Joe's gut gave a sickening lurch, and he didn't know what to think. If he hadn't glanced out of the window as he helped the girls tidy their toys before dinner, he wouldn't have known she was here until the doorbell rang.

Which it was about to do, any second.

The girls had alternated between stormy tears and sub-dued silence all afternoon, and he hadn't been able to leave them with his father. Dad had manned the garage until the last client collected her car, and then he'd closed early. If the phone was ringing off the hook with people wanting service and repair, there was no one in the garage office to hear.

Joe had gone over and over that crazy…and absolutely genuine…proposal of his, and still didn't fully understand where they'd gone off track. Was it the girls? Just the girls? Was it him? Asking for a ridiculous degree of certainty— a certainty that he felt but that she couldn't possibly share. Was he angry with her? Or did he want to give both of them more of a chance?

Okay, here she was, about to arrive, and he didn't have the answer to any of those questions.

He was on his way to the front door before the bell even sounded, having heard her shoes on the brick steps.

"Hi," he said, opening the door and meeting her face-to-face.

"Oh. You saw me."

"I did."

"I didn't want to call first. Well, I should have. You might not have been home…"

"It's fine. I am home. We all are."

"Or you might not have wanted to—" She stopped. She was flushed and it made him want to kiss her. He wished she was flushing *because* he was kissing her, but that wasn't going to happen. Neither of them would know where they stood if he did anything like that, and there was no going back. You couldn't pretend that something like "Marry me" had never been said. Nothing was that simple, and he should know it by now.

This morning, he'd had the brief and utterly clear understanding that marrying Mary Jane would be simple… would make everything simple…but her reaction made it clear that he'd been wrong.

Timing, maybe? Atmosphere?

There should have been flowers or candlelight, not a few harried words in a very practical office. They should have already been in a mood of joy and celebration, not one of anxiety and stress. He'd made her feel that she was a stop-gap measure, a desperate choice with his back to the wall, and what woman would want that?

He was an idiot.

And yet she'd made him feel the wrong things, too— that his daughters were baggage he couldn't expect Mary Jane to handle, that they were an impediment that she would have to overlook, instead of two precious beings for her to embrace.

But still, she was here, and his heart was jumping. "Come in," he said.

She frowned and didn't move. "How're the girls?"

"Dealing with it."

She lowered her voice. "Because that's why I'm here."

"Yeah…?" She was here because of the girls. Wasn't that ironic!

"I—I talked to Penelope." She held up her hand, forestalling the protest he was about to make. He'd told her not to! "Wait, Joe. She's giving them another chance, but I didn't know if you'd want to take it. Maybe you've rethought the whole thing yourself. After all, the trust thing goes both ways. You might not feel they're safe there. I think Penelope herself recognizes that."

"Come in," he repeated, because he couldn't stand having her on the doorstep. He wanted her in the house.

"Should I?"

"I'm asking you to, aren't I?"

"Yes. Yes, you are." She stepped forward and he caught a hint of her scent and it almost brought him undone.

Her stiffness as she slipped past him told him it was too late for regrets, on both sides. She'd pulled right back, and he didn't blame her. He, of all people, should have known that you didn't make radical life plans on a whim. You had to think about these things from every angle. He should be happy that she hadn't just forgotten all about his daughters and said yes purely because the two of them were good in bed. You had to use your brain with this stuff, not just your heart and your—

Yeah, that.

"Let's go in the kitchen and talk," he said, sounding much calmer than he felt. "I need to get dinner going."

"Yep. Sure."

"You can stay for it, if you'd like." After all, she was here because she'd stuck her neck out for the girls. How many women would do that? He wanted her to know how much he appreciated it.

"Well, I…"

"Or not."

"Maybe not."

He tried to inject some humor, to hose things down. "You sensed that it was just hot dogs and oven fries, didn't you?"

She laughed, and that felt so nice. He let go a little. So he'd asked her to marry him in the worst possible way and she'd turned him down because she had more sense than that, but they didn't hate each other, it turned out. He didn't think he could ever hate a woman like Mary Jane. He'd asked too much from her, that was all, and he'd asked it too fast.

"I'm sensing it now," she said as they entered the kitchen, where he had long, garish pinky-red rubbery things thawing on a plate on the countertop, with a packet of matching buns beside them. The really urgent part of the whole operation was the oven fries, because they took longer. He grabbed the bag out of the freezer while she watched, opened it and flung the litter of icy, greasy fries onto a metal tray, then put them in the preheated oven.

"I'm told ketchup is a vegetable," he said, "and I'm counting mustard as a vegetable, too. Potatoes are definitely vegetables, so that's three right there. Arguably."

"Don't apologize for the nutrition. I bet it's been a horrible afternoon."

"It has."

"What do you think, Joe?" Her face tightened. She really cared about this. His gut flipped again. Maybe he'd been wrong. Maybe she hadn't turned him down because of his baggage. So, why?

"What do I think?" His brain was all over the place.

"Penelope will have them back, but do you want them to go?"

He sighed. "Yes, I want them to go. I take your point about the trust issue going both ways, but there are too many good reasons to say yes, and any fears I have about their safety when I think about that stallion, I'll just have to swallow. They love it too much. It's too good for them in too many ways."

"That's why I talked to Penelope."

"You can see it, too."

"Their passion is amazing. You'd said it before and you were right. To harness that. It could be the making of them."

"I signed Penelope's waiver last week, and I haven't forgotten what it said." He quoted, "'I understand and acknowledge that horseback riding is an inherently dangerous activity and that horses can act in a sudden and unpredictable way, especially when frightened or hurt.' But there's another kind of damage you really haven't seen in the girls yet, emotional not physical, and it's there, underneath, and you're right, I think ponies could help heal it."

She nodded, her eyes big and bluish-green and swimming with empathy and care.

"Thank you, by the way," he told her.

"For what?"

"For having sense enough for both of us, today, when I said…what I said."

"When you proposed?"

"Yeah. That." He was deeply embarrassed.

She shrugged and made an odd little shape with her lush, pretty mouth. "It's okay. You're welcome. One of us had to, I think."

"You're right. One of us did. And apparently it had to be you."

As he had done, she took refuge in humor. They were both good at that. "Well, I'm okay about taking that kind of a dive…"

Awkward, awkward, awkward. He wanted to ask if

she'd turned him down because of the girls, but then he thought that he didn't want to hear her say it.

*You were asking too much, Joe, so let it go.*

He said instead, "Let me tell the girls that pony camp is back on. Want to watch?"

"Um, no, I'd better not. Better go."

"Thought you might. It'll be pretty, though. There may be hugging involved. And admittedly, screeching."

She gave a brief smile that didn't quite reach her eyes. "I'd really better go. I'll just say a quick hi to them, and to your dad, if he's around."

"In the shower."

"Oh, well, never mind. Just the girls, then."

"Just the girls," he agreed.

"And you can tell them the good news after I've gone."

And she went.

She went, because it would be too painful to stay.

Mary Jane didn't know which was worse, the spontaneous proposal, or the fact that Joe was apologizing for it just hours later.

What if she'd said yes?

What if she'd done what her heart wanted, and jumped into his arms and screamed out, "Yes, yes, yes!" Would they have been stuck in an engagement that he regretted at once? Would he have gone through with all her pretty fantasy plans, or pulled the plug later on, at the worst possible time, when she'd become even more attached to his daughters and couldn't imagine her life without him or them or the family she wanted so much to create.

Narrow escape, Mary Jane.

She'd done the right thing in turning him down.

The knowledge didn't make her feel any better.

## Chapter Fourteen

Europe appealed. Maybe Scandinavia. There was an amazing-looking hotel in Norway, made entirely of ice, that was freshly built every winter. Now, that would be a unique experience! Or maybe canoeing in Sweden. At the warmer end of the spectrum, there was surfing and yoga in Portugal, or cycling in France.

Mary Jane arrived back at the resort with a whole pile of travel brochures sitting on the passenger seat beside her, most of them featuring vacations that would require several months of fitness training in preparation.

She didn't really want to go on any of them, but she had to do something, have some kind of escape to look forward to, some kind of proof to herself and the outside world that she was okay, and she didn't want to just lie on a beach with nothing to do but think. Travel had always been her go-to activity when life wasn't quite working out right. Rnd if she sometimes didn't enjoy herself that much, it wasn't from lack of trying.

She grabbed the pile of brochures and her purse, climbed out of the car, told herself that she was getting on with her life…and there was Joe, standing right there, three days after she'd last seen him on Friday evening, the day Holly and Maddie had been banned from pony camp and then given their second chance.

"Hi," he said.

"Hi, Joe."

"Need more towels by the pool."

"Right." Since it was the number-one reason anyone came to the office on a sunny afternoon, and since he was wearing swim trunks teamed with a bare, wet chest, she wasn't surprised. The whole sight of him was so difficult and distressing and overwhelming, the bare chest almost didn't register.

She couldn't *let* it register. She didn't need those memories! She was all over the place just seeing him.

She'd been coaching herself relentlessly since Friday, telling herself she'd done the right thing. For herself. For both of them. For the girls, too. Dreams were just that. Dreams. They didn't happen in real life. It was disastrous if you tried to shape your life to fit a fantasy. Hadn't she learned that the hard way with Alex? You had to take control. You had to be sensible.…

*Just run that loop tape one more time, Mary Jane.*

"They usually bring their own," Joe was saying, a little awkwardly, "but we forgot to put them in this morning." He folded his arms across his chest as if he was self-conscious about showing it, and the action made his biceps harden.

They'd slept together. She knew that body so well. She loved it. She wanted it. But she couldn't let herself feel that way.

"I know we're not guests," he was saying, "So I hope—"

"It's fine. You know that, Joe. I crashed your car, remember?"

He laughed dutifully, but they both knew the joke was getting a little stale. He was just being nice. She went to lead the way into the office. The towels were kept in one of the back rooms, and she knew there were plenty. But he was still speaking.

"So… Going away?" He was looking at that big pile of thick, glossy brochures tucked in the crook of her arm.

"Oh, maybe. Just dipping my toe in the water. Something adventurous would be good. Cycling in France, or—"

"Wow," he said. "I'm a little envious. I've barely traveled. Maybe some day."

"Home is nice, too. We live in a beautiful part of the world, and I've had plenty to compare it to."

"You're very lucky."

"Um, yes. I am. I know. I love to get…out…away…" She waved her hand and it fluttered like a moth. His eyes flicked to the movement and then to her face and she knew what he would see there—all the need she couldn't coach herself out of quite yet, no matter how hard she tried. "See new things, meet new people," she added, and it sounded so lame and sad, she wasn't fooling either of them. This was agony.

He called a halt to it, mercifully. "Uh, speaking of toes in water…I really need those towels. They're getting cold." He added uncomfortably, "I wish we could talk."

She felt herself heating up. "Me, too." But he was right. He needed the towels, and she needed to stay strong.

And maybe he was only being polite about the talking. He was holding himself very stiffly, and she struggled to look at him, not knowing where to hold her gaze. She hurried ahead of him, dumped the brochures on her desk and went through to the storeroom to grab a thick pile of towels. Joe waited on the office porch.

When she came back out, she saw two shivering, dripping little shapes picking their way across the gravel, the surface of the driveway too rough for their water-softened feet.

"We couldn't wait, Daddy."

"We're *soooo* cold!"

Joe looked at the towels in Mary Jane's grasp. "Oh, you have a whole pile."

Her arms were full. "To leave by the pool."

"Let me just take the top two." He almost toppled the pile out of her arms and she had to anchor them with her chin—fortunately a skill she'd honed over the years. She and Joe didn't touch at all, just hands on thick fabric. Hands and chin.

He draped a towel around each quivering little pair of shoulders and the scene reminded Mary Jane of that first day the girls had swum here, a couple of weeks ago—was it only that long?

The girls remembered, too. "Can we have hot chocolate today?" Holly asked.

"We haven't broken anything, this time," Maddie pointed out.

Mary Jane didn't know what to say, and Joe seemed to sense it.

"No-o-o, girls," he said at once, sounding reluctant. "Mary Jane is busy."

"Are you busy, Mary Jane?" the girls said in unison.

Mary Jane struggled with herself. It would be so easy to make the offer. She almost bit her tongue, holding it back. There was a silence, just a few seconds, but long enough for the girls to realize that the hot chocolate idea wasn't happening. "I really am busy," she said.

Their faces fell, and she knew she'd lost ground with them, lost favor. She wasn't *always* the fun, friendly lady who'd found a pony camp for them and played mini golf hilariously badly. She was sometimes the busy lady who wouldn't give them hot chocolate even when they hadn't done anything wrong. And who knew what other crimes she might commit in the future, if Daddy stayed friends with her?

They were just children, Mary Jane reminded herself, not angels.

And not hers.

"Must get these towels out to the pool," she muttered. She'd collect the used ones, too. There would be a huge pile.

"Girls, dry yourselves quickly," Joe said, "so we can put the towels in the towel bin, and let's not forget to bring yours next time."

"Just leave them on the porch," Mary Jane told him, and by the time she'd exchanged her piles of towels and said hi to Lucy, Jess and Simon, who were still swimming, his car was on its way up the drive, too far away for her even to wave.

"So do you think the reason Mom and Dad have sprung this visit on us is because they don't trust how we're running this place, and they're checking up?" Daisy asked Mary Jane and Lee.

The three of them stood in the restaurant kitchen, which was clean and quiet at this time of day, following the post-breakfast cleanup, the preparation of lunchtime picnic baskets and the early dinner prep work. It would need to erupt into a hive of activity within the next half hour, however, ready for the evening meal.

Lee simply threw her head back and laughed, but Mary

Jane couldn't take the question so lightly. "Oh, I just bet they are doing exactly that!" she said.

Mom had called from the car, a few minutes ago. "Guess where we are, Mary Jane?"

"Um, Myrtle Beach? Savannah?"

"Saugerties!"

Which was roughly an hour and forty-five minutes from Spruce Bay, on I-87, the direct route up from South Carolina. "You're coming up? For how long?"

"Just a few days. Maybe a week or so. Depending on how things go."

"How things go?"

"You know, the weather…" Mom had said vaguely.

"I knew as soon as she called that they were checking up," Mary Jane told her sisters.

Around two hours from now, Mom and Dad would be unpacking their bags in their old bedroom. Mary Jane had been thinking about stripping it out, redecorating and turning it into her own private space. It was much bigger than her childhood room, which barely had room for the queen bed.

But the Spruce Bay remodel and their parents' retirement to South Carolina had become so tangled in with Lee's and Daisy's personal lives, she didn't feel on solid enough ground to tackle the project yet. She planned on making her own former room into a spare room, so that Mom and Dad would always feel welcome.

It was three o'clock on a Thursday afternoon, and she'd left Nickie in charge of the office and come over to the restaurant so she could alert Daisy and Lee to the impending arrival of the two people who had run this place with modest success and a lot of love for more than thirty years.

Mom and Dad's last visit was two months ago, now, in April, when the resort had been closed, so they hadn't yet seen it in its new summer prime, with all the trees and shrubs thick and green, the annuals in bright bloom, the parking spaces filled and guests enjoying the pool, the barbecue area, the restaurant, the dock, the beach and the boats.

"That's why you came over in such a rush," Lee said. "In case we have something to hide."

"Well, no…"

"Relax, I'm kidding."

"I know, but I'm wondering if we do need to have a meeting before they get here."

"A meeting?" Daisy said. "Is there something you're not happy about, Mary Jane?"

*Where do you want me to start?*

Ugh, that little thread of bitterness was back! And it was made stronger by the fact that Daisy had asked the question so quickly, as if she always expected Mary Jane to be unhappy about this or that.

"Not unhappy," she said.

Miserable.

Over Joe.

*Don't think about that right now.*

She went on, "But I think it's time for some decisions. Cards on the table, or whatever."

"I'll make us an iced chocolate each, shall I?" Daisy suggested.

"Sounds yum," said Lee, who seemed to be constantly starving these days.

Daisy began to move efficiently around, grabbing tall glasses, chocolate syrup, vanilla ice cream and milk. "But keep talking," she told Mary Jane after a minute. "Because I can do this and listen at the same time."

"Okay, well, here goes." She took a big breath. "We're in a bit of a holding pattern at the moment, the way I see it, and it can't last. You both have babies due—" *Careful, careful, careful. Don't make that sound like an accusation.* "—which is fabulous, and I can't wait, but we need to decide how it's all going to work."

She paused while Daisy hit the button on the blender and filled the kitchen with noise. When the machine had gone silent again, and Daisy was pouring iced chocolate into glasses, she went on, "Lee, where are you and Mac going to settle after the wedding? Are you staying in Jay? It's a long way to keep going back and forth, especially once you have a baby. And, Daisy, running the restaurant is a big job."

Currently, Daisy was squirting canned whipped cream with a practiced touch. She never made running the restaurant *look* like a big job, but it definitely was.

"How much time off will you take for the birth? Will you be coming back full-time? I know it's traditionally been a pretty quiet time of year, but we're trying for more of a winter season now…" Mary Jane heard her voice growing increasingly stressed, not to say plaintive, and trailed off. How would they take this?

"We have been thinking about this stuff," Lee said slowly. "Mac and I, that is."

"Tucker and I have been thinking about it, too," Daisy said.

"So…any decisions?"

Daisy presented Mary Jane with her iced chocolate, and said, "We're thinking of buying a house, for a start."

"Oh, wow!" Lee pricked up her ears. "Where?"

"We've looked at a couple along the lake, roughly half-way between here and Reid Landscaping HQ." Daisy and Tucker currently lived in the very nice but not very big apartment over the showroom, which they would have no trouble renting out. "We're working out an offer on one of the houses now," she said, "and talking to the bank."

"So that means—" Mary Jane said.

"It means I'm fully committed to the restaurant. Piri is developing into a great assistant chef, and I have the fall and winter menus planned already."

"Oh, you do?" Mary Jane felt close to tears suddenly. With the three of them all so busy, they hadn't made enough time to talk about serious stuff lately. She'd had Joe on her mind so much, she hadn't realized there was this second undercurrent of concern deep inside her about what was happening at Spruce Bay, or how stressed she'd been feeling about it. What would happen if Daisy wanted to leave?

"Yes!" Daisy said, "Have you been worried about it, Mary Jane?"

"A little."

"Don't be. I've been making notes about the menus for weeks. I'll be testing the recipes out over the next couple of weeks and locking in prep methods and ingredients so we have it all going smoothly before I need to stop working. There's no reason why Piri can't manage the place while I'm off. Our other staff all want as much work as they can get, and they seem happy here."

"That's great!"

Lee took a long pull on her iced chocolate, through the pink plastic straw. "Things are a little different at my end," she said slowly.

Daisy and Mary Jane both looked at her.

"I love Spruce Bay in a personal sense. We had such a great childhood here. Every stick and stone seems precious to me, but Mac and I have realized it's not right for me as a career. It's not a career at all. I don't have your management skills, Mary Jane, or your vision for the place. Or your creative passion for cooking, Daisy. I'm just filling in where I'm needed, and too much of it is indoors. You know how I love to be out in the open air."

"So what are you saying?" Mary Jane asked slowly.

"I'm saying you could replace me with any twenty-something woman or man who's happy to work hard and do anything that's needed. You'll find someone easily."

"You're leaving, then?"

"Mac and I are looking at buying a place, too—the house we're renting in Jay, in fact, because the owners have told us they plan to put it on the market soon. It's pretty and sweet and easy to manage, and a great base for us with his job at Whiteface. I'm not sure how much time I'll take when the baby's born, or if we'll try for another baby fairly soon. We like the idea of two. But when I do go back to work, I want it to be in the area I love—skiing and rock-climbing and mountain-guiding." She screwed up her face. "What do you think, girls?"

"I—I have to say I'm not surprised," Mary Jane said. And she knew Lee was right. She hadn't been doing the kind of work around the resort that would make her hard to replace.

"We'll miss you, Lee," Daisy told their middle sister.

"It's not far for visits," Lee reminded them. "It's only far when I'm trying to commute several times a week. Mary Jane, how does all this sound to you? Are you happy about it? Does it fit in with your plans? I mean, you and Joe…" Lee spoke carefully and she was frowning, as if she suspected she might be treading on difficult ground.

"That's…not happening anymore," Mary Jane said, and felt the change in atmosphere at once—the tactful silence, the sympathetic disappointment.

*Single again? Bad luck, Mary Jane!*

Should she have told them sooner? It was nearly two

weeks, now, since she'd gone to Penelope to beg for a second chance at pony camp for Joe's girls, and ten days since he'd caught her with that sheaf of travel brochures in her hands when he'd come looking for towels.

They'd seen each other several more times here at the resort, when he'd come to drop off Holly and Maddie in the mornings, or pick them up at the end of the day. He'd said hi and they'd talked, and each time the talking had lengthened a little beyond the polite exchange Mary Jane had initially planned.

Each time, she'd felt shaken up and miserable for hours afterward, finding every word they said to each other and every expression or piece of body language stupidly important and precious.

Each time, she'd wanted to offer hot or iced chocolate to the girls, so that they didn't think she was mean, and each time she'd resisted. She thought Joe had begun to notice it, too.

Her sisters were still looking at her, wondering about him.

Lee began, "But, Mary Jane, you looked so—" She stopped.

"What?" Mary Jane prompted gently. "Say it. I'm not that fragile."

"Good together. Happy about him."

"It's—it's fine."

"What happened? Can I ask?"

"I think I was interested for the wrong reasons."

"Yeah, well, that body of his could drive most women to a rash reaction, I admit," Lee drawled. She was way off base.

"That's—that's pretty much it, I guess," Mary Jane lied through her teeth, because she didn't want to talk about the real reason.

*I didn't trust myself. I was trying to turn fantasy into reality, and it doesn't work.*

"Anyhow, Lee," she went on superbrightly, "you asked if I was happy about your plans, and Daisy's, and I am. Incredibly happy. I knew you couldn't have been totally satisfied with working here, Lee. I was scared you'd decide to go back to Colorado and I wouldn't get to watch your baby grow. And, Daisy, if you want the restaurant to be totally your domain, I couldn't be happier. It'll become a dining destination for the whole region, I bet, and it means I can concentrate on the rest of the resort."

"I'm going to cry," Daisy announced suddenly, and her voice cracked and went foggy on the last word. "I'm sorry, it doesn't make sense. Must be the hormones. But it seems as if we've got everything sorted out and we're all happy about it, and Mom and Dad will be happy, too."

"I think so," Mary Jane said. "Which is good, because they'll be here pretty soon."

"You were right. We needed a meeting." Daisy hugged her suddenly. "You're a good person. And you are *smart!*"

Mary Jane hugged her back then shooed her away, because it was all a little too much right now. She could easily have made her pregnant-and-hormonal sisters look like models of emotional control, by comparison. "You're always hugging me in this kitchen, Daisy."

"So shoot me. Kitchens are very emotional places for me."

"I'm crying, too," Lee said, wiping her eyes. "That is *sooo* out of character. Don't anyone dare tell Mac, or he'll use it against me."

"So, united front from the Cherry sisters when Mom and Dad get here?" Daisy said.

"Absolutely!"

Their parents arrived on schedule at four forty-five.

Mary Jane heard the car peel a little too fast into the parking area in front of the office and knew it was Dad because he always did it, with Mom reminding him that there could be children around so he should slow down.

She went out to meet them…just as another vehicle came down the drive—Joe's minivan. He'd come to pick up the girls. She waved at him as he drove by, heading for a spot closer to the pool, because the girls were splashing and shrieking in there with Simon and Jess. The late-in-the-day swim had become a regular part of their pony-camp routine, and they hadn't forgotten to bring their towels lately.

"Who was that?" Mom asked as soon as they'd hugged. She was still watching Joe as he climbed out of the minivan and called a greeting to the girls.

"Oh…Mr. Capelli's son."

"Mr. Capelli from Capelli Auto?"

"That's the one."

"Which son? Didn't he have a few?"

"Joe. He was in my year."

Dad hugged her, too, then said, "He's staying here at the resort?"

"No, he's not."

"Then why are his kids in our pool?"

"It's complicated. It's not important."

But Mom and Dad were both a little too keen on micromanagement, and insisted on hearing the full story.

They didn't *get* the full story, of course, but they got the public part of it—the Richardsons, and pony camp, and Joe being a single dad and running the garage while studying for the New York bar.

Dad looked across at the pool, where two dripping, dark-haired peas in a pod were toweling themselves under Joe's firm direction, making Mary Jane's heart kick. Maybe she should have offered hot chocolate…. "Hmm," Dad said. "Sounds as if he's turned out pretty well."

So Dad approved.

Mary Jane's heart kicked painfully inside her rib cage.

All part of the fantasy—her parents beaming at her engagement party and wedding, calling all their friends to announce their new grandchild.

*Not happening, Mary Jane.*

Mom was watching Joe and the girls now, too, and both her parents' attentive interest seemed to mock Mary Jane afresh. "They look like two little bits of mischief," Mom said.

"Oh, they are! Very energetic. Joe does a great job with them."

Mom looked at her, and Mary Jane could almost see the speculation in her eyes. So the man was a single father, huh?

"Let me get your bags inside," she said very briskly, and to her profound relief, the subject dropped.

Last day of pony camp tomorrow, and the Richardsons were checking out of their cottage first thing Saturday morning, in order to load up their horses and start the long drive back to Kentucky. After tomorrow, Holly and Maddie wouldn't be coming to the resort anymore.

After tomorrow, Mary Jane could start getting over Joe, instead of looking for him morning and afternoon, and falling apart every time they spoke.

## Chapter Fifteen

After tomorrow. But tomorrow hadn't happened yet.

In the morning, Mary Jane saw Joe bringing the girls to deliver to Lucy and the Richardsons for the last time, while she and Mom and Dad ate Daisy's restaurant breakfast out on the big, extended restaurant deck. Taking herself brutally in hand, she looked away from the sight of those familiar skinny little-girl legs in riding jodhpurs and those bright backpacks bulging with snacks and water bottles and swimming gear, shepared along by such a caring set of arms and such broad shoulders.

"Do you like the cranberry coffee cake, Mom?"

"Oh! Are you kidding me? It's to die for!"

So far, the Cherry parents had been full of praise and approval about the changes at the resort and the way it was running. This was in contrast to last Fall, when they'd found it quite difficult to let go, and to believe that anyone else could really care about the place as much as they did, or manage everything so well.

Dad was still a little grumbly at times. "Do people really want coffee cake for breakfast?" He'd ordered scrambled eggs, bacon and home fries, himself.

"Well, judging by how fast Daisy usually sells out of it, yes!"

"I guess this was why it was time for us to retire," Dad said. "We just weren't up on the trends. I never would have remodeled the bathrooms in those colors!"

"But they look great," Mom said quickly. "So don't keep saying it, Marshall. You've seen the new bathroom colors about five times since they were done."

Today they planned on driving up to Jay to see the house that Lee had told them she and Mac were going to make an offer on. They were staying up there for a home-cooked meal in the evening. "Home-cooked by me!" Mom had said. "Lee looks as if she needs to start putting her feet up more." Daisy had given them the addresses of the two places she and Tucker were considering, also, and they intended to drive by those and sneak a look on their way.

Mary Jane's own plan to do a big redecoration of the master bedroom and claim it as hers seemed small-scale by comparison, but she'd decided to take herself in hand on that front, and once Mom and Dad had left for their house-appreciation drive, she spent her spare moments during the day browsing the internet for bedroom decor that she liked…as well as looking at those damned travel brochures. She was leaning toward Portugal in March.

At five-thirty in the afternoon, Nickie was staffing the office for the evening, so Mary Jane went out into the fresh summer air to make her daily—sometimes it was twice-daily—inspection of the boats, checking that no one had left life jackets inside them, or puddles of water, making sure there were no oars missing, damaged sections that might spring a leak, or boats missing altogether.

It was a beautiful day, so quite a few people had taken the boats out, and she wasn't sorry to have a good reason to come down to the dock. The lake was so pristine and peaceful on this part of its long shoreline. A scattering of islands meant that the big tourist boats didn't come too close, and no matter what the weather or the time of day, the play of light from sky to water to rock to trees held something magical.

Mary Jane took deep breaths of the pine-scented air and told herself she was content. Happy. Fulfilled. Going to be an auntie soon. Lucky enough to live in this beautiful spot. Sensible enough to have said no to Joe two weeks ago. He must have thought so, too, because he hadn't called or reached out. There'd only been that exchange over the towels, and those increasingly awkward talks whenever they accidentally met.

You couldn't grab at something just because it looked like the thing you wanted. What was that thing Dad so often said? "If something seems too good to be true, it probably is."

True, Dad could sometimes be a bit of a gloomy-guts and a worrier—witness his reaction to coffee cake for breakfast, and his oft-repeated skepticism about the new colors in the bathrooms.

*It's beautiful. I'm happy. I'm doing the boats. I always like doing the boats.*

There were clear instructions sign-posted about the boats in four places on or near the dock. "Please leave dinghies and canoes upside down, with oars and paddles inside. Please return life jackets to the office."

Still, almost every day somebody didn't read the signs, or couldn't be bothered. You had the choice of enforcing such a strict policy with taking the boats out that no one ever did it at all, or mentally shrugging and accepting that you needed to check them. Today, Mary Jane found one boat with four oars while another had none, and there were two canoes sitting on their bottoms with a slosh of water inside, and soggy life jackets floating in the slosh.

Meanwhile, dinghy number three wasn't even back yet. She looked out at the lake and saw it coming round the point of one of the islands, only just close enough for her to make out that it was indeed a sky-blue-hulled Spruce Bay boat. The occupants were just three tiny blobs of life-jacket orange.

She lifted the sopping jackets out of the two canoes in front of her, keeping them as far from her body as she could, so that the water would stream onto the ground and not on her skirt, top or sandals. Really, the outfits she wore in the office were never the right clothes for checking boats, but it was too much trouble to change.

Flipping the boats was worse than lifting the life jackets, in terms of mess, especially when the water was three-inches deep. Fortunately, as always, she'd brought a bucket for bailing. This made the boats lighter to flip, but tended to result in getting water all over her. She bailed anyhow. Scoop, splash. Scoop, splash. It was still sunny and warm. The splashes down her clothing would soon dry.

But it was amazing how much water one boat could hold.

Scoop, splash. Scoop, splash.

"Need some help?" said a male voice.

It was Joe, wearing bare legs and puffy orange on top, standing two yards away and looking down at her. There was a half smile on his face that she couldn't read. Pleasure, and uncertainty, and awkwardness, and...

She gulped down her gasp of surprise and blurted, "Oh,

that was you and the girls out in the last boat?" It was pulled up onto the sand about fifteen yards away, but they were still sitting in it, trying to work the heavy oars with lots of giggles and not much success.

They were too cute!

And Mary Jane hadn't let them have any hot chocolate. She looked quickly away.

Flustered.

Emotional.

Breathing turned shallow just because Joe was here. Would she manage to hide it? This was a much more private place than any of their other recent meetings.

"Sorry, are we late back?" Joe's smile hovered and flickered, and made her heart do stupid things that she didn't want. It made her smile back at him, too, and there was this fuzzy moment…long moment…when all that mattered was that he was here, robbing her of breath.

"It's fine," she said unsteadily.

"Lucy took Jess and Simon in from the beach a while ago, so they could help pack. It was our last day." He began to unfasten the garish life jacket, and soon had it dangling from one hand. Beneath it, he wore a striped polo shirt, with wet patches all over it.

"I know," Mary Jane said. "I bet the girls are disappointed."

Somehow the content of this conversation seemed totally unimportant. They were both looking at each other as if they couldn't drag their gazes away.

If their chance conversations over the past couple of weeks had been awkward, this was worse. It was already intense, despite the outwardly casual words.

"They would be sad," he was saying, "but Penelope says they've learned so much that they're good enough riders to take part in another camp she's running in August for two weeks. Meanwhile, they'll have a riding lesson with her twice a week, and I've found another day camp they can do until the August one starts."

"So your dad won't get too tired, and you'll have study time, and the girls have more ponies to look forward to. That's great!"

"Yeah, it is." He gave a brief grin, but then it faded and the atmosphere grew thick and uncertain again. "Uh, I got here early and the girls asked if they could have a boat ride for our last day. I hope that's okay. We're not guests, after all."

The girls had scrambled out of the boat now. They arrived and stood beside him, wearing smaller versions of the orange that Joe had worn, their chins almost buried inside the bulky life jackets. They were in swim gear, and only now did Mary Jane see the pink-and-blue backpacks and bright beach towels the girls had left in a heap at the foot of a tree twenty yards from the dock and beach.

She would have recognized those backpacks if she'd noticed them before. She would have been prepared. As it was, she felt caught on the hop to a stupid extent, not calming down at all, and had a horrible awareness of how little she was managing to hide. The girls weren't smiling. They weren't at all sure about her, anymore.

"No, it's fine," she repeated. "Of course it is."

"Fine, we're not late back, fine, it's okay that we're not guests, or fine, you don't need help?"

"Either. Both. I mean, all three."

"I definitely think you need help. Look at you!"

She stood up and looked. Enough water splashed on her cream top to make it semitransparent, telling Joe and anyone else that she was wearing a pink bra. She should have changed. "Um, yes," she said, and positioned the bucket so that it shielded her damp chest from his quite unapologetic gaze. She knew she was blushing.

"Don't do that," he said softly.

So she gave him the bucket, without a word. Even though it might not have been the water bailing he was talking about. Their hands met, clumsy and cold and wet and perfect. She snatched hers away. The girls were looking on with interest, now. "Are you embarrassed because your underwear is showing?" Holly asked with a child's bluntness and disregard for tact.

"A bit."

"Girls…" Joe said. The breeze took his protest and floated it away.

"Can we help, too, Daddy?"

He seemed harried at this idea. "No, why don't you take the life jackets off and dry yourselves and play in the sand? Over there." He pointed to a spot farther away than it needed to be.

"Are we staying?" Holly asked.

"You said we had to go home," Maddie reminded him.

"We're staying a little while."

"Yay-y-y!"

"And didn't you say you were hungry? Maybe we'll eat your snacks in a few minutes."

"Okay." They scampered off, and Joe looked relieved.

"You don't have to bail water for me," Mary Jane told him.

"What if I want to?"

"Then…then…okay."

He got down on his hands and knees beside the most water-logged of the boats and began to bail, scooping and tossing the water in one continuous figure-eight movement. Mary Jane wanted to tell him again that he didn't have to do this, but no words came. It was too good. The way he worked so efficiently to help her. Had any man ever done this for her?

He was showing off a little, she could tell, and so help her, she loved it.

Loved what it said.

That in some way he still cared. He hadn't dropped out of her life or turned his back or lost interest completely just because they'd gone too far, too fast with their involvement and overshot the whole thing, only to have it come crashing down.

*Maybe he doesn't think we messed up for good, after all.*

Or else he was just a good, decent guy, still grateful to her for what she'd done to help his girls, and prepared to show it.

Well, that wasn't quite so good, not quite so personal and intimate and important, but she valued it anyhow. She'd learned that in life. So you can't have the big things you want? Value the small things. Value what you're sure of.

"Thanks so much, Joe," she finally managed to say.

"No problem. This one, too?"

"And then they need to be flipped."

"You do this every day?" he said as he bailed.

"The guests are supposed to do it, but often they don't."

"So you do, instead? On your own?" He bailed some more.

"When there's no one else. Dad always used to do it before he and Mom retired to South Carolina. Daisy and Lee aren't in a fit state to help with this stuff because they're both pregnant."

"You don't have to tell me! Lee has a basketball in there!"

"She's due sooner. Daisy still insists she can flip boats with me, but I won't let her. When Rick, our maintenance man, is around, I get him to do it, but he only works part-time and he often finishes too early. People take them out late when it's this light and warm."

"You need someone full-time for that kind of stuff, not part-time." He finished and stood up. There was only a half inch in the bottom of the boat now, so it would be easy to flip.

"This is our first summer since Mom and Dad left," she told him. "We're still working things out."

"You need someone," he repeated, and his glance flicked down at her chest again. Looking at the wetness, possibly.

Or possibly not.

She blushed once more, a happy, uncomfortable blush that she didn't know what to do with.

*Keep it together, Mary Jane. Breathe. Be sensible. Don't read too much into this. Don't read anything.*

Don't give too much.

Want too much.

Expect anything.

Together they flipped the two boats. She moved on to the one he'd just brought back, but he wouldn't let her. It was surprisingly dry inside, and she guessed he'd been fairly strict about the girls rocking and splashing. He called them. "Holly, Maddie, we need to flip the dinghy."

"It's okay, Joe, we can—"

"Hey, I can read, even if some of your guests can't. We take a boat out, we're supposed to leave it flipped and re-turn the life jackets. Girls?"

They came running back from the swimming beach, and he got them to stand at one end and lift on the count of three. Mary Jane suspected he could have done it more easily by himself, but he was strict about things like that, she'd noticed—tidying toys when they'd finished playing, bringing empty plates into the kitchen when they'd eaten their meal.

"Can we play more?" they asked when the dinghy was lying facedown on the sand.

"Yes, go on." He dropped his voice. "If you have time, Mary Jane?"

"If I have time?"

"I want to talk a bit." His eyes seemed so dark with feeling that she could have drowned in them, and his voice was pitched so low that she had to step closer to hear. "There's something I need to ask you about what happened two weeks ago."

"About—"

"You know what about." One flick of his gaze made his meaning clearer than words could have done, but he spelled it out anyhow. "Why you said no. I have to ask. Was it because of the girls? I can't let this go. I've been thinking about it ever since. The three of you seemed so good together. They talk about you. They like you."

"They didn't seem to like me last week when I told them they couldn't have hot chocolate."

"I wondered about that, too. I saw you hesitate."

"You let me off the hook, saying I was busy."

"And you grabbed the excuse," he reminded her.

"I—I guess I did."

"You have to tell me straight. Are they too much for you to think of taking on? Was that why?"

"No! No, Joe!" It shocked her that he needed to question this. "That's not it at all!"

He barely seemed to hear. "I mean, it's a deal-breaker for both of us. You must know that."

"Of course I know it! Of course you wouldn't want to be involved with a woman who wasn't interested in your children! And how could any woman with any integrity take on someone else's children if she didn't find a way to care about them?"

"So if it's not them that you don't want…"

She made a desperate, last-ditch bid for honesty, because if she couldn't be honest with this man, then what hope did she have? "Joe, it's the opposite."

"The opposite?"

"When I said no to you that day, it was because I was afraid I wanted them too much. Wanted a ready-made family too much. Want one, still. I was afraid about how easy it seemed when we came together. You have the life to offer that I've always wanted. I'm…greedy for it."

"Is that bad?" He came closer and reached for her. "Surely that's not bad?"

She folded her arms once more into their protective position and shook her head. "Greed is not a good basis for anything, is it?"

"You don't strike me as a greedy person. Like you just said, the opposite."

"There are different kinds of greed. Different ways to be needy." She couldn't meet the look in those dark eyes, now. Couldn't unfold from her defensive posture, even though he was running his hands over her shoulders and down her arms. This was such a confession. That she was so needy and hungry, not just for a man, and lovemaking, but for a family and a nest. "I can't shoehorn you and your girls into my fantasy of a family life. And that's my problem, not yours or the girls'. I want it too much."

The oldest reason in the book for driving a man away, and yet she was saying it, admitting to it. He would run a mile.

So far, he wasn't. "Hey… Is that really all it is? You don't doubt me or the girls at all, you only doubt yourself?"

"That's enough, isn't it?"

"No! It's nowhere near enough! It doesn't count at all."

"What does count, then? Help me, Joe, I'm so confused. It seems so complicated. I'm fighting so hard with myself—"

"I can feel that," he said softly. "You're fighting me, too, trying to stop me from kissing you." He pressed his mouth to her hair. "And it's not working—" to her temple "—at all." She make a helpless sound of surrender and lifted her face so that he could find her mouth.

"What do I do, Joe?" she said between the soft, plummy, seductive touches of his lips.

"Just stop. There's no need to fight. It's not complicated. It's simple. This is *right*. That's why we've both been feeling so bad for the past two weeks. That's why whenever we've seen each other we've just wanted to stall and stall so we could keep talking."

"Oh, you too?"

"You didn't notice? You did, but you were too busy making it difficult and impossible and wrong for yourself, in your head, which made me confused and I thought I had to pull back. Don't do that, Mary Jane."

"No?" she whispered.

"No. Please," he whispered back. "Just love me, like I love you."

"Just that?"

"Yes, that. It's not greed for a dream. I can't believe that. Not when I feel it so strongly. It's real."

Her heart began to fill. "I do love you. I love you so much. And the girls."

"That's everything, that's all that counts, and we both need to trust it, and go where it leads, and if you don't want me to talk about marriage, yet, if that still scares you, then I won't."

"No, Joe?" she whispered.

"We can leave that." He smiled at her, held her, kissed her again. Were the girls watching? There'd be some explaining to do very soon… "You wait, Mary Jane Cherry. You just wait. I'm going to spring it on you, down the track, in some impossibly romantic setting that will blow any other guy's proposal out of the water. You'll never see it coming, and you'll be powerless to resist."

"You don't have to wait," she told him shamelessly. "You can say it right now."

"Yeah?"

"I'm not sensible today. I'm admitting total defeat. If you want to marry me, then I want to marry you, and I don't care how or where you ask me."

"As long as it's now?"

"Right now."

"Marry me, Mary Jane?"

"Yes, please."

"That sounds so good…"

"What sounds good?" Holly said, trotting to within earshot.

"Why are you hugging Mary Jane?" Maddie asked.

They both looked suspicious, eyes narrowed, lower lips stuck out. Mary Jane wanted to lavish hot chocolate on them right now, and anything else their hearts desired, but she knew she couldn't. She had to take her cue from Joe. This wasn't a dream, this was real life, a future with two little girls who'd been damaged in the past and who needed careful handling. It would be a lot of work. She would get it wrong sometimes. She wouldn't always be their best friend.

"Because we've just had a talk," their dad said. "And we've decided we're going to be a family."

"How? When?" They both began hopping up and down. They weren't quite sure yet why this was exciting, but

Joe's attitude told them it was, so they reacted accordingly. "A *family*?"

"A family. People who care about each other, and share each other's lives, and do good things for each other, and know and promise that they always will. That's a family, girls. Wanna start this minute, with a granola bar picnic on the dock, the four of us? I think I have a spare bar for your new mom."

"Our *mom*?" shrieked two identical voices.

"Does that sound good?"

"Yes!"

"It sounds really good!" Holly yelled. "Good, good, good!"

A little hand sneaked it's way into Mary Jane's, and she felt Maddie's quieter presence beside her. "Does that mean we can play with your makeup now, Mary Jane? Please, please, pretty please? If you're there helping us, and we're so, so careful not to drop it?"

"Don't say yes," Joe muttered to her in a stern aside. "This is the thin end of the wedge."

"Are you joking?" she muttered back.

"Yes, I'm joking," he said. "You can let them play with your makeup if you really want."

"I—I think I do." She was overwhelmed, giddy, happy, daunted, all at the same time.

"You're crazy, sweetheart."

"I know." And the only thing that stopped her from bursting into tears was Joe's arm tightly around her, telling her that beyond all the shifting, ballooning emotions in her heart, everything was good.

## *Epilogue*

Waiting for the results on the New York bar exam was a little like waiting for a baby to be born. You were given a rough date on which to expect the event, but there were no promises or guarantees. Coincidentally, Daisy's baby girl was due in mid-November, which was exactly what the New York Board of Law Examiners had announced about when they thought they might give out the results of the July exam.

By early November, Daisy was getting pretty antsy and fretful about the whole late pregnancy thing. She'd complained more than once, "I'm so huge! I'm bigger than Lee was, I'm sure of it! What if the baby's late? Can I really stand another four weeks of this? How big is that baby girl going to be?" And then she'd apologized for complaining and disappeared into the bathroom to take an antacid tablet for her heartburn.

She definitely wasn't making the last few weeks of

pregnancy look like a fun experience, and if it wasn't for Lee and Mac embarking on parenthood in a bright light of happy energy, Mary Jane might have been wondering why she was so eager to experience pregnancy herself.

Lee and Mac had had their baby boy on the twenty-third of September, two weeks before Mary Jane and Joe had their quiet, low-key, but completely perfect wedding, with two identical flower girls. Her love for Joe had gone on feeling right from the moment she'd said yes to him, and she didn't want her wedding to feel like a public parade of success. It needed to be quieter than that, a personal celebration of joining their lives, and acceptance of the challenge and responsibility and joy.

Mary Jane had moved into the Capelli family home on North Street, so as not to disrupt the girls with another move, or to leave Joe's dad without help. This left the Cherry family apartment above the Spruce Bay office empty for the first time in thirty years, but assistant chef Piri was keen to rent it, and would be moving in any day.

Lee's baby, Adam, was a darling, adorable little boy, now six weeks old and already smiling, and to Mary Jane he seemed like a promise about her own future. She and Joe weren't using any contraception, and she couldn't wait to find out if something had happened this month. She should have a pretty good idea within the next couple of weeks.

But for Joe, his dad, the girls and Mary Jane herself, the thing she was most on tenterhooks about was the result of the bar exam.

Every day when the girls came home from the new school they'd already settled into, they asked him about it. "Did you find out about the exam yet, Daddy?"

"Not yet."

His dad would greet Joe and Mary Jane after they'd

been for an evening out with the news, "I checked your email. Nothing's come through yet."

"Well, it's still earlier than their average, according to what they say," Joe would calmly reply.

"2012 results came out on November second, you said."

"We're not in 2012."

Of all of them, Joe seemed like the most stoical and restrained about the whole thing, and Mary Jane loved him for it. She knew how he'd learned to be that way—through all the months he'd had to wait for court dates and assessments from children's services—and she knew how hard those life lessons had been.

So when she first began to suspect that she was pregnant, she didn't know what she should say. Tell him about her hopes, when they were still so tenuous and uncertain? Or wait until she had more reason to be sure? Wait till they knew if he'd passed the bar?

She let four more days go by. So did the New York Board of Law Examiners, and, very tetchily, so did huge, uncomfortable Daisy.

The girls were at school, Joe's dad was raking leaves and Joe was at the garage when Mary Jane finally cracked and went to the drugstore to pick up a test. An hour later, Art was taking a nap, and Joe had just walked in after picking the girls up from school.

He kissed her and she took in a breath ready to say...

"Let me just take a look at something," he muttered before she could speak. He disappeared into the little room off the dining room where he studied and kept his computer, and she knew exactly what he was doing.

Mary Jane stood there, biting her thumb, while the girls ran into the kitchen to see if there was something to eat. They continued to have voracious little appetites but never seemed to put on weight. There'd been a few confrontations over toy tidying and vegetable eating, but there were so many precious moments, too. Mary Jane felt her love for them growing day by day, and it seemed as if the tired, defiant, difficult episodes from the girls were what really deepened it. Right now, they weren't being tired or defiant, they were oblivious, and so was Joe.

When he came out of the computer room, she was determined to get in first.

But she didn't. Because the news was obvious in every line of his body.

"Guess what?" he said, and he was grinning from ear to ear. "I passed the bar exam!"

Mary Jane burst into tears and threw herself into his arms. "Oh, Joe!"

"Are you proud?"

"Incredibly! But not surprised. Not for a second. I knew you would."

"That's my girl."

"And guess what?" Now she was grinning through her tears. "I took a pregnancy test just now…"

Joe whooped so loud that the girls came running, and Art's footsteps could be heard upstairs, heading this way, so the news didn't stay private for long. That was fine. They were a family. Five of them now, soon to be six.

When the phone rang a little later, while everyone in the Capelli household was still giddy and chatty and happy, Mary Jane picked it up and somehow wasn't all that surprised when she heard Daisy's husband, Tucker's, voice. He was phoning from the hospital, sounding weary and proud and relieved and happy. "Guess what?" he said.

* * * * *

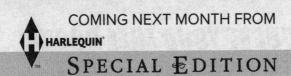

# COMING NEXT MONTH FROM

## HARLEQUIN®

# SPECIAL EDITION

## Available January 21, 2014

### #2311 ONCE UPON A VALENTINE
*The Hunt for Cinderella* • by Allison Leigh
Shea Weatherby isn't interested in love, but millionaire playboy Paxton Merrick has taken quite the human interest in this journalist's life story. When Shea finds herself pregnant after a passionate night with Pax, she must decide if she'll let down her guard for true love.

### #2312 A SWEETHEART FOR JUDE FORTUNE
*The Fortunes of Texas: Welcome to Horseback Hollow*
by Cindy Kirk
Cupid hit cowboy Jude Fortune Jones right in the heart when he met Gabriella Mendoza. But the lovely Latina is hiding a secret—she's a heart transplant patient and might not be able to have children. Can the rancher romance his lady to a happily-ever-after?

### #2313 THE REAL MR. RIGHT
*Jersey Boys* • by Karen Templeton
Single mom Kelly McNeil seeks refuge from her ex. In the process, she runs into her best friend's brother, hunky cop Matt Noble. Kelly and Matt forge a close bond, but she doesn't want to give up her newly found independence for him. Can Matt teach her how to love again?

### #2314 REUNITING WITH THE RANCHER
*Conard County: The Next Generation* • by Rachel Lee
Returning to Conard County for her beloved aunt's funeral, social worker Holly Heflin can't avoid her ex, rancher Cliff Martin. Sparks ignite between them, but Holly is headed back to Chicago in two weeks. The city girl and the cowboy wonder if it's worth resurrecting the past to create a future....

### #2315 CELEBRATION'S FAMILY
*Celebrations, Inc.* • by Nancy Robards Thompson
Widower Dr. Liam Thayer isn't looking for romance—least of all at a charity bachelor auction, where Kate Macintyre bids a hefty sum on the single dad. As Liam and Kate begin to fall in love, she begins to wonder whether she can ever truly be a part of his family.

### #2316 THE DOCTOR'S FORMER FIANCÉE
*The Doctors MacDowell* • by Caro Carson
According to Dr. Lana Donnoli, her ex-fiancé, biotech millionaire Braden MacDowell, prefers profits over patients. When Braden returns home, he and Lana are thrown together over an accident, where they find that the past doesn't always stay there...and this time, "fiancée" might turn into "forever."

---

HSECNM0114

# REQUEST YOUR FREE BOOKS!

## 2 FREE NOVELS PLUS 2 FREE GIFTS!

### ⊕ HARLEQUIN®

# SPECIAL EDITION

## Life, Love & Family

**YES!** Please send me 2 FREE Harlequin® Special Edition novels and my 2 FREE gifts (gifts are worth about $10). After receiving them, if I don't wish to receive any more books, I can return the shipping statement marked "cancel." If I don't cancel, I will receive 6 brand-new novels every month and be billed just $4.74 per book in the U.S. or $5.24 per book in Canada. That's a savings of at least 14% off the cover price! It's quite a bargain! Shipping and handling is just 50¢ per book in the U.S. and 75¢ per book in Canada.* I understand that accepting the 2 free books and gifts places me under no obligation to buy anything. I can always return a shipment and cancel at any time. Even if I never buy another book, the two free books and gifts are mine to keep forever.

235/335 HDN F45Y

| | |
|---|---|
| Name | (PLEASE PRINT) |

| | |
|---|---|
| Address | Apt. # |

| | | |
|---|---|---|
| City | State/Prov. | Zip/Postal Code |

Signature (if under 18, a parent or guardian must sign)

### Mail to the **Harlequin® Reader Service:**
**IN U.S.A.:** P.O. Box 1867, Buffalo, NY 14240-1867
**IN CANADA:** P.O. Box 609, Fort Erie, Ontario L2A 5X3

**Want to try two free books from another line?**
**Call 1-800-873-8635 or visit www.ReaderService.com.**

* Terms and prices subject to change without notice. Prices do not include applicable taxes. Sales tax applicable in N.Y. Canadian residents will be charged applicable taxes. Offer not valid in Quebec. This offer is limited to one order per household. Not valid for current subscribers to Harlequin Special Edition books. All orders subject to credit approval. Credit or debit balances in a customer's account(s) may be offset by any other outstanding balance owed by or to the customer. Please allow 4 to 6 weeks for delivery. Offer available while quantities last.

**Your Privacy**—The Harlequin® Reader Service is committed to protecting your privacy. Our Privacy Policy is available online at www.ReaderService.com or upon request from the Harlequin Reader Service.

We make a portion of our mailing list available to reputable third parties that offer products we believe may interest you. If you prefer that we not exchange your name with third parties, or if you wish to clarify or modify your communication preferences, please visit us at www.ReaderService.com/consumerchoice or write to us at Harlequin Reader Service Preference Service, P.O. Box 9062, Buffalo, NY 14269. Include your complete name and address.

SPECIAL EXCERPT FROM

**H** HARLEQUIN®

## SPECIAL EDITION

*Jaded journalist Shea Weatherby isn't interested in romance—least of all, with a man like millionaire playboy Paxton Merrick. Shea falls pregnant after a passionate night with Pax, but she can create a real family with a bad-boy bachelor?*

\*\*\*

"You've got more experience to put on your resume now. If you really want to leave, do it."

She made a soft sound. "Probably not the best time for job hopping."

"Being pregnant, you mean." His soft words brushed against her temple and his thighs moved slowly against hers.

She exhaled shakily. "Mmm-hmm."

"You wouldn't have to work at all if you didn't want to."

She shook her head, though rubbing her cheek against the warmth radiating from him was probably the real motive. She forced herself to stop. To lift her head so there was at least one part of her not plastered against him.

She realized he'd danced her farther away from the others than she realized. "I'm not going to be your kept woman, Pax, if that's where you're heading."

His head lowered and she felt his lips against her cheek. "Baby mama doesn't fly for you?"

She slowly shook her head.

"What about wife?"

Something inside her chest fisted.

Beatrice had warned her he'd head that direction.

She pulled back again as far as his arm surrounding her would allow, which wasn't far. "Getting married just because I'm pregnant is a bad idea. We already agreed."

"I didn't agree," he said quietly. "I just didn't choose to debate the issue with you."

She didn't know why she was tearful all of a sudden. Only that she was, and there was no way he could fail to notice. "Please don't do this here," she whispered thickly.

He lifted one hand, touching her cheek gently. "Shea."

Tenderness from him would be her undoing. "You're supposed to be celebrating your best friend's wedding," she reminded.

"I'm celebrating my best friend's *marriage*. Anyone can have a wedding. Erik and Rory are going to have something a lot more important. Something that lasts a lifetime."

"And maybe they'll get there," she conceded huskily. "Right now they love each other, at least. They're starting out with a better reason than pregnancy."

His feet stopped moving altogether, though he still held her close. "Why is it so hard for you to see what's right in front of your face?"

Her throat felt like a vise was tightening around it. "I don't want us to end up hating each other."

Despite the dim lighting, his eyes searched hers, leaving her feeling raw. Exposed.

"There's no rule that says we will."

\*\*\*

*Enjoy this sneak peek from*
USA TODAY *bestselling author Allison Leigh's*
*ONCE UPON A VALENTINE, the latest book in*
THE HUNT FOR CINDERELLA *miniseries.*

# HARLEQUIN®

# SPECIAL EDITION

**Life, Love and Family**

Don't miss the final chapter of the Celebrations, Inc.
miniseries by reader-favorite author
Nancy Robards Thompson!

Widower Dr. Liam Thayer isn't looking for romance—
least of all at a charity bachelor auction, where
Kate Macintyre bids a hefty sum on the single dad.
As Liam and Kate begin to fall in love, she begins
to wonder whether she can ever truly be a part
of his family.

*Look for CELEBRATION'S FAMILY
next month from Harlequin® Special Edition®,
wherever books and ebooks are sold!*